Finnish Russian Border Blurred:

A Noveramatry

A combination of novel, drama and poetry all in one line

Affectionately dedicated to

UUU
U
U
UUU

who believe there is no skin between us

Special thanks to

Marja Jussila

for her insightful reading of

an earlier draft of this book

Mehdi Ghasemi

Finnish Russian Border Blurred:

A Noveramatry

A combination of novel, drama and poetry all in one line

Finnish Russian Border Blurred: A Noveramatry

A combination of novel, drama and poetry all in one line

Text Copyright © 2018 by Mehdi Ghasemi

Cover and interior design: Mehdi Ghasemi

Front cover photo: Mehdi Ghasemi

Back cover photo: Jonne Renvall

Publisher: BoD™ – Books on Demand, Helsinki, Finland

Manufacturer: Books on Demand GmbH, Norderstedt, Germany

ISBN: 978-952-80-0593-3

Con10ts

List of Correctors:

Me; later Juho

The Girl; later Olga; later Sanna

The Internet

The Barber

Minna

Alexander

The Phone

Someone

The Boss

The Book

The Mom

The Old Woman; later Satu

The Man

The Woman

Sirkku

Setting

Area: T.here

Era: Now and then

Di.vision 1
Pas & Dance

I saw her for the first time on the Silja Symphony dance hall while cruising between Helsinki and Stockholm. She looked charming, and a single sight sufficed to smite me with her charms. I could not take my eyes off her while she was dancing professionally on stage. I was sitting in the last row of the dancing hall, sipping my drink. How can one be so gorgeous?! It seemed that God had used all His|Her skills to create her.

Even during the concert hiatus, I was disconcerted by the hiatus of her bod and thought. My eyes could not help chasing her, and thus, I eyed her at all times. After a short break, the concert restarted with the song "You're My Heart, You're My Soul." Immediately, she went on the stage again and burned up the dance floor! I badly wanted to dance with her, but I was he.sit.ant. Hesitancy can k.ill opportunities and leave us live with remorse! I did not see the courage to approach her and ask her to dance with me; however, I had to shake a leg if I wanted to have her.

I long for her, but I'm shy!

        Why, WHy, WHY!? I shall die!

I need all streams to run after me

        And a storm to sink my bash in a sea

Step out of your cave, man

        You can, YOu can, YOU can!

After many internal conflicts, I stood up, but still my legs were not ready to take me to that stage. I dragged myself, but for every two steps that I took fore, I took one back! After an age, I reached the dance st.age, stood in front of it and fixed my eyes on her. I was starving for her at10tion. She was dancing a.l.one, but in fact, I was dancing with her in my own hall.ucination.

For a second, our lOOks tied together. I was staring at her, and she was staring back! Perhaps she needed a partner, or perhaps she had detected my love. All of a sudden, she b.linked and stretched her right hand toward me. I could not believe my eyes! I didn't know what to do! I could h.ear the beats of my hear.t h.ear.t in my ears. Boomp, BOOmp, BOOMP! If continued for 10 more ticks, blood had been pumped out of my veins! Faintheartedly but joy.full.y, I stepped on the stage!

Me
My goodness! I'm dancing with her! How would it be possible? Am I dreaming?

The Girl
What?

Me
Nothing!

The Girl
What's your name?

Me
Juho.

The Girl
Sorry the music is loud, and I couldn't hear you! What is your name?

Me
Juho.

The Girl
Joho?

Me
No! Juho.

The Girl
I see!

The Girl
Where are you from?

Me
Finland!

Sweat was running down my body, but my throat was dry. Too much bash is a d.anger.ous thing, and I was confident that she would feel disappointed with me in 10 seconds. I didn't want to lose her after all, so I tried to regain my forces. I cleared my throat.

Me
What's . . . *your* . . . name?

The Girl
Olga.

Me
You . . . are from . . . ?

The Girl
Russia.

Me
Which . . . city?

The Girl
I was born in St. Petersburg, but now I live in Pushkin. Do you know where is Pushkin?

Me
No!

The Girl
It's not that far from St. Petersburg.

Me
Aha!

Olga
How about you? Where do you live?

Me
Tampere.

The Girl
Tamper!? Where is *Tamper*?

Me
Not Tamper! *Tampere*. It's a city . . . in . . . southern Finland.

The Girl
I see!

Talking to her made me calm down and adapt my moves with hers.

Every now and then, I cast a furtive glance all over her appealing body. Her blue eyes, blonde hair and white skin had spellbound me. She was adorable!

The Whole of Me

To you, I offer the whole of me
I'd like you to be in my destiny
To you, I offer every atom of my soul
For I believe that you and I can be we

I have fallen deep for you
I see myself in your eyes blue
The radiance emitting from them
I hope never ever go through!

I wish I could freeze time. I did not want our pas and dance to end, but time is a regular traveller and flies like butterflies. Before long, the concert was over, and the dance stage was empty from maddening crowd, but we were still there. Suddenly, she stretched her hand, and we shook hands.

Olga
Very nice to meet you!

Me
Yah, yah!

Olga   **Me**
Me   **Olga**
Olga   **Me**

Olga
Good night!

Me
Night!

She walked away. After a short while, I walked behind her slowly. She carefully went ⬇ the stairs toward cabin floors, and I followed her furtively, lest she not.ices me. I had no contact information of her, and if I lost her, then I would curse myself for the rest of my life. She entered the long corridor of C cabins, and a while later, she stopped in front of a cabin, searching for something in her handbag. My cabin was there, too, and this gave me confidence to shake a leg and approach her.

Me
Hello again!

She suddenly turned back toward me.

Olga
Hello!

Me
Is . . . your . . . cabin here?

Olga
Yes! Where's yours?

Me
Right here.

Olga
Really?! So we are neighbors! What a coincidence!

Me
Yes! I really . . . . enjoyed . . . meeting . . you . tonight!

That was the longest sentence I had uttered since meeting her! How a shy boy like me could go that far with a pretty lady?! That was the main reason that had left me a.l.l a.l.one in my w.hole en.tire l.ife. Who knows? Perhaps I have been lucky to be alone all these years as the hand of destiny had destined to offer me a better choice! The hand of destiny sometimes wittily and subtly knits!

Olga
It's a mutual feeling!

I cleared my throat.

Me
Would it be . . . possible . . . to . . . have your . . . phone number or . . email address?

All my body was wet with sweat! What if she says, "NO!"

Olga
No problem! Do you have a pen?

Me
Just a moment!

I started searching for a pen in my pockets, and she did the same in her handbag. Eventually, I found a pen, and she found a piece of paper.

Olga
Write! olga.fillipov1@yahoo.com

Me
o l g a . f i l i p o v 1 @ y a h o o . c o m. Is that right?

Olga
No, fillipov has double ll.

Me
I see. Thanks!

Olga
You're welcome!

Me
Good night.

Olga
Good night!

She entered her cabin and closed the door. For a few seconds, I was in a shocking mode! I had been baffled as if I was not in this world!

It took me a little while to get my five senses back. I entered my cabin! What an idiot I am! Why did I end that sweet conversation with a "Good night?!" I am a fool, an idiot, a dumb! That's all! Why didn't I add some coal to the fire of our conversation and make it go on and on and then invite her to have a drink?! What does she think of me? A shy reserved nervous boy, who doesn't know the ABC of flirting with girls and winning their h.ear.ts! I wish I was more skilful. If so, there was no wal|l between us now!

I had a terrible feeling. Bit by bit, a headache came through, and I just lay down on my bed and closed my eyes. I wanted to bang my head against the wall. Why am I so reserved? Is it genetic or what? How can I change myself?

10

All her images, words and moves passed through my eyes nonstop. I had saved them in *mine* mind. My temperature was high, and I could feel it. I dried the cold sweat of my forehead with the back of my hand, relentlessly cursing myself. I stood up and walked around my small ca.bin like a frenzy, who had no control over himself. I felt like a single encaged bird that had lost its mate and banged itself into its cage walls. I moved my head constantly with regret, but that could not change anything.

I wished I could remove the wall between our cabins and make them one. I wished I could have her.e tonight. I had lost my mind. Once I was reading a post on Facebook, saying sometimes we just complicate our life. We can call someone whom we've missed. We can invite those whom we wish to meet. We can state what we dis.like. We can ask for whatever we wish to receive, and we can notify those whom we love. However, we make this simple equation complicated with a reserved attitude.

Suddenly, I stood up and decided to go and knock on her door. I looked at myself in the mirror|rorrim. My forehead was hot, and my cheeks flushed as if all my blood had been pumped into my head. I touched my ears. They were burning as if they had been in an oven for 10 minutes. Anyway, I had made my own mind. I opened the door and entered the corridor. I stood in front of her cabin, took a deep breath and stretched my hand . . . . but then, I became he.sit.ant! What shall I say after she opens the door? Shall I invite her to have a drink together? What shall I do if she refuses? Isn't she in bed now? These questions generated doubt in me again. I totally lost a little courage I had tried to pump in myself and felt like a flat tire again.

Desperately, I returned to my own cabin and lay down on my bed, but wandering thoughts did not let me sleep. I was frequently moving from side to side. Sometimes I sat up, and sometimes I stood up, walking around the cabin. I wish I could sleep smoothly just like her. Love k.ills! Love rubs our hearts and minds!

I looked at my watch. It was 10 past five. I thought this is not the end of the world. I might see her tomorrow morning again if she does not get off the ferry when we arrive in Stockholm. Sleeplessness was torturing me, so I closed my eyes.

After a while, I heard someone knocking on the door. Up I got. Who's that? I looked at myself in the mirror|rorrim. My hair was a bit messy. I tried to line them up quickly with my hands. Then, I hurriedly opened the door.

Olga
Good morning!

Juho
Oh my God! Look . . . who is here! Come on in, come on in!

Olga
OK! Thanks!

I lost my head again, and all of a sudden, I was all thumbs! I did not know what to do! I just moved from one side of the cabin to the other side clumsily, and one could easily notice that I was extremely stressful! I had lost my confidence.

Juho
Welcome!

Olga
Thanks!

Juho
Please . . . take . . . a . . . seat!

She grinned from ear to ear. I was still shocked! Why has she visited my cabin at this time of night? Whatever her intention, I was happy to have her in my cabin, but how could I start flirting with her. All of a sudden, a question came to my mind:

Juho
How . . . old are . . . you, Olga?

Olga
Guess!

Juho
30?

Olga
30?! Do I look so old?!

Juho
No, no! I . . . mean 25?

Olga
No!

Juho
23?

Olga
No, but you are getting closer!

Juho
20?

Olga
Yes! How about you?

Juho
I'm 32!

Olga
32?! I don't believe it! You look younger!

What an idiot I am! Why did I start the conversation with a question about her age with 10 years difference! Communication is a skill, but I don't have it. What the heck! I wish there were some courses on communication skills!

Juho
Do you want something to drink?

Olga
No, thanks!

I lOOked at her lips. They suddenly moved me! Her red rose lipstick had made them kissable! I sat next to her. She smelled like daisies! Then, I put my hand around her waist. She showed no reaction! I looked at her lips again and moved my head closer to hers and started kissing her! Incredible! How could I do so? How could I go that far so fast?!

While kissing her passionately, I heard some noises outside the cabin. There were some people walking quickly, talking together and carrying their luggage in the corridor. Their noises awakened me! I jumped out of the cabin to see if Olga is still there! The door of her cabin was wide open, and I could clearly hear someone moving inside the cabin. I peered into her cabin delightfully, but to my great surprise, she was not she! She was a cleaner, tidying up her cabin! She had left the ferry, and what she had left for me was a memory and an email address.

I had to return to Helsinki by the same ferry. I had a horrible cruise. She had badly stuck herself in my mind. I re.member.ed every second of my dream deferred. What if it had come true!

During the cruise, I was both sleepy and depressed. However, her thoughts did not let me sleep. I went again to the dance hall. There was no performance, and it was empty. I fixed my gaze on the spot whereon we danced together. I could visualize every single moment of it. I had saved all her moves in my mind, and now my mind was replaying them.

Di.vision 2
Piece & Miss

I arrived home at about 10 pm. I was starving, but I had no energy to cook anything. My mind was still oscillating like a pendulum between the dance stage and her cabin. I thought I would faint soon, so I dragged myself to my kitchenette, opened the fridge and took out some raspberry yoghurt.

I got a part of my energy back. I went to my desk and switched on my computer. It was as slow as a slug, and it took me about 10 minutes to come up. Then, I scratched the username and password off a new internet card and entered them. The dial-up noise was scratching my soul! It took a while until I was connected.

Immediately, I opened a google page and entered her name. The pictures of several women appeared on screen. I went through all of them carefully, one by one, but none of them was my soulmate; I mean the one who had kindled a fire in my heart that all the waters of the seas could not put out! Then, I opened a yahoo page and attempted to log in to my email account. It took me years to log in. I checked my internet speed, and it was 64 kbit|second; however, I estimated it to be no more than 10 kbit|second!

The Internet
Trust me! My loading rate is 64 kbit|second, and I am doing my best, but if you have high expectations, ask my inventors to improve me.

Juho

Please be a bit faster. You have never been in love, and you can't understand me!

After a lot of struggle, I opened a new email page and started writing:

```
-------------------------------------------------------------------
To: olga.fillipov1@yahoo.com
-------------------------------------------------------------------
Cc:
-------------------------------------------------------------------
Bcc:
-------------------------------------------------------------------
Subject: Silja Line
-------------------------------------------------------------------
Dear Olga,
It was nice meeting you last night on the Silja Line. I hope to see you soon again.
Sincerely Yours,
Juho Siltamäki
```

I was excited! What else can I add to it? I thought, but nothing more came to my mind. I sent the email as it was without being able to add any word to it. However, right after sending the email, I was engaged in an internal conflict.

Juho

"Hope to see you again?" So what?! When? Where on earth? Why am I always so telegraphic? Why can't I express my feelings? There is no word count limit for the expression of feelings, and I do not need to pay for it. Why do I expect others to understand what I really feel? Is that a type of poverty? A poor person lacks money, and I lack words to express my feelings!

I logged in to my email account 10 times a day for about 10 days to see if she had replied! The low speed of internet had made me frustrated. Despite that, I did it frequently, since her love had made me blind. No reply. What shall I do? Shall I send her another email and ask for her phone number?

Juho
The Internet

He   sit   ant   ly, I decided to send her another email. I opened my email box and started writing:

```
----------------------------------------------------------------------
To: olga.fillipov1@yahoo.com
----------------------------------------------------------------------
Cc:
----------------------------------------------------------------------
Bcc:
----------------------------------------------------------------------
Subject: Silja Line
----------------------------------------------------------------------
Dear Olga,
I am Juho, and I write to say how much I enjoyed meeting you on the Silja Line about 10 days ago.
I wish to see you again either in Finland or in Russia. Since you might check your emails less often,
may I ask for your phoone number?
Truly Yours,
Juho Siltamäki
```

Right after typing it, I became hesitant to send it.

Juho
What does it mean to send two emails one after the other?! That's not good at all. What does she think of me? Let me save this as a draft and wait for a couple of days, but would it be a *waiting for Godot*?

The Internet
No! Send it!

Juho

I can't! She might think . . .

The Internet

She might think what? People can think whatever they wish. The fear of what people think of us makes life a jail and limits our thoughts and deeds. People look at you differently; some look at you positively and some negatively. Some find you attractive, while some others find you repulsive. Some might love you, and some would abhor you. While some people look down on you, some others honor you. So don't let people's views stop you. Do whatever you should. Stop hesitancy and take action! Your first email did not include any question, so why do you expect her to answer it?

Juho

So ... shall I send it right now?

The Internet

Yes! Send it!

I went through it quickly and made some small changes to it.

To: olga.fillipov1@yahoo.com

Cc:

Bcc:

Subject: Silja Line

Dear Olga,

I am Juho, and I write to say how much I enjoyed meeting you on the Silja Line about 10 days ago.

The meeting was brief but extremely enjoyable for me. I wish to see you soon either in Finland or

in Russia. Since you might check your emails less often, may I ask for your phoone number?

Truly Yours,

Juho Siltamäki

I closed my eyes and pressed the SEND button. Right after sending it, I reread it, and unfortunately, I found a spelling error!

Juho
Oh no! Why this happened?! Why did I mistype the word "phone?"

The Internet
That's not a big issue.

Juho
That's not a big issue?! It seems that you do not take everything seriously! This is too bad, especially in the first contact! What does she think of me now? She might think that either my English is poor or I am careless!

The Internet
You have already sent it, and nothing can be done! So you'd better take a deep breath and keep calm!

Juho
Ok, but will she reply?

The Internet
Don't worry!

I was really starving, so I went to the kitchenette and made a sandwich for myself. After gobbling up my sandwich, I brushed my teeth and went to bed. I just moved from side to side but could not sleep. I counted her eyelashes while lying down, and I wished that I had her.e now, touching her soft blonde hair and whispering some compliments in her ears!

Days flew by, and I didn't receive any reply. I was getting sure that she wouldn't reply my email. Perhaps, she has no connection either to me or to internet, perhaps she has a boyfriend, or perhaps she has given me a fake email address. Was her name really Olga Fillipov? If not so, where on earth can I find her? If I had had a silver tongue, I would have owned her! Desperately, I decided to find a girl bearing some resemblance to her in Tampere. While walking in streets or visiting public places, I looked at girls around myself to see who resembles her the most.

Once I visited my regular barber to cut my hair. Upon arrival, The Barber told me that he has to leave, and if possible, Minna, his new colleague, would cut my hair.

Juho
No problem!

I sat down on a chair, waiting for Minna to appear and start her job. Suddenly, I looked back in the mirror|rorrim and saw Olga standing right behind me! Up I got!

Juho
Hey Olga!

The Barber
Olga?!

Juho
Yes, she is Olga. We met on the Silja Line a couple of weeks ago! She knows me pretty well! Don't you?!

The Barber
Olga|Minna
The Barber

22

The Barber
But she is Minna!

Juho
Are you sure?!

Minna|Olga	The Barber
Juho	Juho
Minna|Olga	The Barber

The Barber and Olga|Minna exchanged some looks full of astonishment.

The Barber
Yes!

I turned back and browsed Olga|Minna more carefully. It seemed that I had goofed! I went speechless, felt hot and started sweating!

Juho
Sorry!

Both Minna and The Barber smiled crookedly. I sat ↓, and The Barber left. Minna put a white sheet around my neck and fixed it. Then, she gave me some tissues to dry the sweat off my face. While I was drying my face, she went and turned on the radio. I didn't dare even to raise my head and look at her in the mirror.

Minna
How would you like it to be?

My mouth was dry.

Juho
Taper fade.

Minna
What do you mean?

Juho
I mean . . . taper . . . down from longer . . . hair at the top . . . and get thinner . . . towards my neck.

Minna
I see.

She started her job, while I was looking down. I was embarrassed. What a fool I am!

Soon the job was over. I hurriedly paid, and as soon as I left the place, I took a deeeeeeeeeep breath. I was still sweating, so I dried my forehead with the back of my hand and headed for home. Olga had haunted|hunted me! I sought for her everywhere! Her thoughts had badly affected my job and personal life! I wish I could either find her or lose her; otherwise, life would be unbearable.

Di.vision 3
Pace & Space

I got up early in the morning, took a shower, had a brief breakfast and headed for my workplace. I decided not to check my emails anymore as I had turned into an emailoholic, and it had negatively affected my life.

During the noontime, I warmed up my lunch, went back to my office, closed the door and sat in front of my computer. The dark monitor was right in front of me, and that enticed me to turn on the computer and log in to my email account. I tried to resist, but I failed. While waiting for the computer to boot up, I twirled and pushed some spaghetti with a fork into my mouth, and while waiting for my email account to open up, I finished my lunch. Eventually, my inbox popped into view, and I saw her name!

UP I jumped and dropped the fork!

Juho
Oh my God! She had replied! How would it be possible?

I put my hand on my heart. Icouldeasilyfeelitsfastbeats ^^^^^^^
Hurriedly, I clicked on her email, but it took me a while to open! Every second passed like 10 hours! I wished I was a computer expert and could improve its speed! No choice, I had to wait. Finally, it opened, but as soon as I wanted to read it, someone knocked on my office door!

Juho
Ah!

In one tick, I put my lunch box in a drawer and closed my email box. Then, I stood up and opened the door nervously. My boss along with a stranger were right in front of the door.

The Boss
Hello Juho!

Juho
Hello!

The Boss
This is Alexander.

I stretched my hand and shook hands with him reluctantly.

Juho
Nice to meet you!

Alexander
Nice to meet you, too!

The Boss
Alexander is based in St. Petersburg, and he is willing to export and sell some of our products to Russia. He is back to Russia today, so have a meeting with him right now and see how we can work together.

Juho
OK!

The Boss left, and I invited Alexander in. I briefly introduced our company, and he introduced his firm and demands. Several times,

I wanted to ask him whether he knows someone, called Olga Fillipov, but that could be a foolish quest.ion, since half of Russian girls are named Olga, and the other half are Fillipov!

Juho
So I prepare a draft based on our today's agreements, and after receiving The Boss' confirmation, I will send it to you for your observation by Friday.

Alexander
Great!

Juho
Have a safe trip!

Alexander
Thanks! Bye!

As soon as he left, I logged in to my email account again. It took me about 10 minutes to reopen her email. The email read:

To: Siltamäki Juho <juho.siltamaki10@yahoo.com>

Cc:

Bcc:

Subject: Re: Silja Line

Dear Juho,

Thank you so much for your emails and sorry for getting back to you late. I do not have regular access to internet here. Here is my home phone number: 0078121011.

Looking forward to talking to you soon,

Olga

The Internet
What would you like to do now?

Juho
I'll call her.

The Internet
Call her!? How about me? I made you connected together, but now you wanna leave me out and call her!?

Juho
What else can I do when she has no regular access to you!

The Internet
This is not fair! You betrayed me! One day, I will be so strong that you cannot live even for a tick without me, and even phone calls will be done through me! Remember this moment!

Juho
Really!? I don't believe it!

The Internet
You'll see. I have learned to be stronger wherever and whenever I feel neglected! This is the only remedy! One day those who have ignored me will make a dramatic plea to have me!

I read and reread Olga's email several times, word by word, letter by letter. Does she love me, too? If not, why did she reply my email? Does she want to hold a relationship with me? If no, why did she give me her phone number?

I returned home. It was dark and chilly, but I felt light and warm and wanted to run from Tampere to Pushkin nonstop. What love does to us? It's a strong drive. It can make impossible possible, hard easy, clumsy clever, ugly pretty and long short.

28

O Love!

You are a strong force

You are a robust source

You can ill and kill

And mill a high hill

You can rise dead bones

And change them to hormones

O Love! I hate you!

Your rosy flames burn me like a single oat

Your tempests agitate me like a small boat

Your winds move me like a joyful kite

And make me fly in sky in the sunlight

O Love! I love you!

As soon as I arrived home, I went toward the phone. I tried to dial her number, but I had a lot of stress. I knew if I call her at this time, I would ruin everything. All of a sudden, due to the high level of stress, I got a sore throat and could not speak clearly. I had a scratchy feeling in my throat, and I could not even breathe properly! My mouth was dry, and drinking gallons of water didn't help!

I sat down and thought! Imagine, I call her right now! What do I have to say? I shall probably start with umm_____
I had no idea! How some men can properly use their silver tongues to look charming?! Why my tongue is so short and does not contain even one gram of bronze, let alone silver?!

After a lot of thought, I desperately found that I had nothing to say! So I decided to call her some other time. To start is always the most difficult part of everything. I went to bed but could not sleep. I decided to watch some movies. Perhaps I could grab some ideas from their dialogues. I turned the tele.vision on and quickly changed some channels until I saw a man and a woman talking together in bed. I had no idea what was the movie about. I lis10ed carefully to what they said:

The Man
Is there anything wrong with me?

The Woman
No, nothing serious!

The Man
Nothing serious?! What do you mean?

The Woman
I don't wanna talk about it now!

The Man
My nightmares are about losing you, baby! It's scary!

The Woman
The truth is . . . I gave my heart to you, the whole of it, and you smashed it!

The Man
Me?!

The Woman
Yes *you*! I wish I knew how to quit you, but without any heart, I won't last long!

The Woman   The Man
The Woman   The Man
The Woman   The Man

The Man
I don't know what you are talking about!

The Woman
That's why I didn't wanna open the valves of my heart to you, but remember that love can sometimes ruin everything. It can break hearts. It can destroy minds. It can . . .

The movie could not help me at all, at least not at this stage! Perhaps I need it sometime later, so I turned the tele.vision off. Sleeplessness k.ills! I remembered a Japanese legend saying that if you cannot sleep at night, that's because you are awake in someone's dream. So am I awake in her dream?!

My mind was busy thinking what to say and how to win her heart with a phone call, but I had no idea! Several days went by, and I still had no idea how to start and what to say! I spent some time in a public library, perusing some books to get some ideas.

Eventually, I decided to call her. My heart was in my mouth, beating faster than ever. My mouth was dry, but the palms of my hands were wet. I dialled her number, and with every digit I dialled, my heartbeats became faster. I could not breathe deeply.

Someone
Здравствуйте.

Juho
Hello! This . . . . is . . . Juho . . speaking.

My voice sounded soar, so I tried to clear my throat.

Someone
Какие? Я не могу понять тебя!

Juho
I want to talk to Olga?

Someone
что ты говоришь?

Juho
Olga?

Someone
Сейчас Ольгу нет.

Juho
I wanna talk to OLGA.

Someone
Olga?

Juho
Yes!

Someone
Сейчас Ольгу нет.

She hanged off. I stood up and looked at myself in a mirror|rorrim. I had become red as a beetroot. I didn't understand her at all. Who was she: her mom or sister? Had I dialled a wrong number or what? I had become bewildered!

I decided to dial again later. Perhaps this time I manage to talk to Olga herself. I counted every tick tack of the clock. Waiting is a sign of true love, and the longer you wait, the more you appreciate what or whom you earn.

I picked up the phone and started dialling, but then I became indeterminate and started thinking that perhaps it would be too late to call her now! Is there any time difference between Tampere and Pushkin? I went to my bookshelf, opened my calendar and found that the time difference between Helsinki and St. Petersburg is about 1 hour, meaning it was 10 pm over there!

The Phone
Call her right now! It's not late now; tomorrow would be!

Juho
It's late! Perhaps she's in bed!

The Phone
Love knows no time! Don't shilly-shally! Go ahead! Hesitancy kills your opportunities and makes you live with regret!

Juho
Juho
Juho

The Phone tried to prod me into calling her, but I was of two minds. I hemmed and hawed for a while, and finally, I put the receiver back on its cradle. The Phone is right. Hesitancy is a killer.

I went to bed, and I had another sleepless night! I wondered how long a man could survive without sleep! This love had ruined my peace of mind. She had really spellbound me.

Di.vision 4
Permit & Port

In off.ice, I made a draft based on our agreements with Alexander and sent it to The Boss for his notice. I returned home early. I was sleepy and decided to take a catnap. I went to bed and tried to sleep, but I had trouble falling asleep. Then, I tried to change my sleeping position, but it was of no avail. How could I sleep when I knew that I would talk to her soon? I was determined to call her, so I got up, went toward the phone, picked up the receiver and dialled her number. With every digit I dialled, I had my heart in my mouth!

Olga
Здравствуйте!

Juho
Hello! This . . is . . Juho . . speaking.

Olga
Joho?

Juho
Yes, Juho! I wanna talk to Olga!

Olga
This is Olga!

My tempo suddenly rose!

Olga
Thanks for calling!

Juho
Juho
Juho
Juho

Olga
Juho?! Do you hear me? Are you still there?

Juho
Yes!

My mouth went totally dry just like a hot desert.

Olga
How are *you*?

I could feel her warmth from that long distance! Her soft clear lovely voice was full of vim, and that started charging my dead battery!

Juho
I'm . . . fine . . . . How . . about . you?

Olga
I'm fine, too!

I was done! I had nothing else to add or ask! That's the w.hole of me: laconic!

Olga
Tell me about yourself!

Juho
I . . . live in . . Tampere, and . . . . I'm a sales clerk. How . . . about you?

Olga
I'm a university student here at Pushkin University. I study biology. I love music, dance and travelling. I live here with my mom and younger brother. My father died in an accident about 10 years ago when my brother and I were just kids. My brother is a high school student. My mom is supportive, caring and kind. You should see them. Would you like to visit us here in Pushkin?

I was super excited to hear that! Oh my goodness! That was what I wished for!

Juho
Really?!

Olga
Of course! Do come over any time you wish! We can also tour around Pushkin and even St. Petersburg.

Juho
My plea.sure!

Olga
Good to hear that! Just tell me when you can make it!

Juho
Sure! I'll check . . . my calendar . . . and let you know.

Olga
Fine! See you soon then.

Juho
See you. Good night.

I was relieved! I felt I was as light as a feather. I dressed up and went out jogging! What a great feeling I had! Her words had energized me and made the cloudy sky of my heart serene! It would be great to see her again. How warm she was! Her warmth attracted me just like a magnate attracting a nail. She further glued my heart to hers!

I went to a lake near my house. It was getting dark, but two swans were still floating on the soft waves of the lake. I wish she was sitting next to me, but . . . . Perhaps I was not that far to make that dream come true!

Early morning, I contacted a travelling agency, which was somehow close to my workplace and asked about a short trip to Pushkin. The agent said that Finnish citizens need a visa to enter Russia, and I should apply for it from the Russian consulates in either Turku or Helsinki. She also recommended me to travel by train from Tampere to St. Petersburg and then from there to Pushkin. However, I needed to change my trains three times in Helsinki, in Finland|Russia border and in St. Petersburg. I had never imagined that it might be so demanding to reach my soulmate even for a short period!

I called the consulate of Russia in Helsinki and asked about the required documents. Based on what they said, I needed an invitation letter and a hotel booking confirmation! I also learned that the visa processing takes about 10 days! I had to call Olga again, informing her how it should go!

Olga
Здравствуйте!

Juho
Hello . . . Olga! Juho is calling.

Olga
Hello Juho!

Juho
Today I . . . called the consulate of Russia, and they said that . . . I need an invitation letter . . . and a hotel booking confirmation . . . for visa application.

Olga
No problem. I send you an invitation letter and a hotel booking confirmation. Do you want to receive them by email or by fax?

Juho
Email.

Olga
Ok! I will send them to you by email. Please let me know if you need anything else.

Juho
Sure! Bye!

Olga
Bye!

As soon as I hanged off, I started thinking why I am so blunt. She kindly said that she would send the documents to me, and I had to thank her, but instead, I cut the call short and said, "Bye!" I remembered every word I uttered and analysed them one by one! Sometimes I sweated while thinking about my own words! I shall change! I shall learn how to start a conversation, how to smoothly fan its fire and how to end it politely. I started reading some books to improve my conversation skills. Those skills could be used in my negotiations with my customers, too. However, I soon found that some of the suggested techniques merely looked good on page but not on stage! I mean they looked nice in word but not in action.

I received the invitation letter and the hotel booking confirmation in a couple of days! So prompt! Does it signify her attention and affection toward me?! She had booked me a single bedroom in a hotel, named Natali, from May 1 to May 10. For 10 days?! How could I stay there for 10 days?! My boss would not agree!

I sent her an email. First, I acknowledged the receipt of the documents. Then, I thanked her for the time and energy that she had spent on receiving and sending the documents. This is something that I had forgotten to do on my phone call. Then, I asked about the length of my stay. She then replied that the exact date of my stay can be modified after receiving my visa, and then, I can stay as long as I wish. Accordingly, I sent the required documents to the consulate of Russia and applied for a visa.

It took me about three weeks to receive my visa. Immediately, I visited that travel agency and asked them to book some train tickets for me from Tampere to Pushkin. They looked through different times and dates, and based on different train schedules, I made my mind and decided to stay there for three days. I booked my tickets and returned home bright-eyed and bushy-tailed! I called Olga and notified her of my visa status and the exact dates of my trip. The news of my trip caused a stir in her, too. I was also bouncing off the walls! What would happen in this trip? Will I win her heart? Shall I . . . ? Something inside me suggested to hold my horses! First, I need to know her well and build a strong relationship with her!

I counted the days. I remember that I used to be an eager beaver in my workplace – first to arrive & last to leave! Not anymore! Her love had made me a daydreamer! I was always thinking of her, checking my emails 10 times a day, thinking of what to buy for her and her family, reading love stories and keeping some key words and sen10ces in mind to use and look romantic!

Without love,

                    Life is dull as a stagnant pond,

Waveless!

                    Like a dry yellow leaf on a path,

Windless!

                    Life but would ebb and flow,

With lashing love,

                    Like a wavy windy roaring sea.

I still had 10 more days to go, but I had already packed up! However, I had trouble finding some gifts for her and her family. What to buy? This one? No! She might not like it. That one? No! It does not look Finnish. These ones? No! She might not like their colors. Those ones? No! They look cheap. I had no idea what to buy! By the way, that was our first real meeting, and my gifts would affect her and her family.

The Book
It is not the gift that counts, but the thoughts behind it!

Juho
In reality, most people count the value of gifts!

The Book
It depends!

Soon it was time to depart. I took a shower, shaved, put on some perfume, dressed up to kill and excitedly went to the Tampere train station. I arrived too early. At the station, I lOOked at people and tried to guess what they were thinking of. Some looked neutral, reading books or papers! Some had grim faces, and I could read sorrow in their eyes, while some others tried to hide their joy. Perhaps they were meeting their beloved. Unlike them, I had joy and couldn't hide it. I smiled, and some people looked at me strangely!

The Book
Juho
The Book
Juho

My train soon departed, and in a few hours, I found myself at the Helsinki main train station. After an interval, I got on another train to the Finnish|Russian border. There, all passengers got off the train and walked through a long corridor, which seemed to be the 0 border. I just followed them. Barbwires and yellow warning signs had made the zone look intimidating! Soon, my joy was replaced by anxiety. I got nervous and broke out in cold sweat! Russian soldiers' stern eyes, unsmiling faces and machine guns made my blood run cold. I was holding my breath. A Russian soldier shouted something out in Russian, and some people passed over us and rushed out to the front. Then, I found that they first would process the Russian citizens and then the *other* nationals. We who remained behind lined up - In about one hour, it was my turn to enter a cabin. I didon't have a good memory of *cabin* of any type! Cabin signifies:

sepa|ration	space	seclusion
singlehood	silence	segregation

While entering the cabin, the soldier\|policeman sitting in his checkpoint kiosk scanned me with a keen observation and then asked for my pass.port. He gazed at my pass.port and lOOked at all its pages one by one. Then, he probed my visa and stared at my face. I was restless! He wanted me to leave my hand luggage there and leave the cabin.

I had a lot of 10sion! Why did they seize my passport and luggage? What would happen if they rfuse to return them? What would happen if they de.port me? What would happen if I miss my train? Is there anything fishy about me? These questions and a lot more p.assed my mind over and over again! While standing in a corner, I opened my book and continued reading it. At least, it could help me pre10d that I had no ants in my pants! I read a paragraph, but I did not understand even a sen10ce of it!

The Book
If you can't stand the heat, get out of the kitchen!

Before long, a soldier|policeman appeared with a couple of luggage in one hand and some passports in the other. He called some Finnish names in a funny accent, and a few people stepped forward and received their luggage and passports. After a few minutes, another soldier|policeman appeared. I saw my luggage in his hand and that made me tranquil! He called my name and handed in my passport and luggage.

I looked at my watch. Oh no! My train would depart in a few minutes! Hurriedly, I ran toward the station. An old train was there waiting for us to board! I got on the train, and it took me a few minutes to find myself back!

I eagerly looked out of the window. I was curious to see how Russia looks like. I could detect a great difference between here and there. There was only a borderline, but that had made a great difference! One line and this much difference?! I did not believe my eyes! I only crossed a line, and the whole distance between here and there was about one kilometer, but the difference was about one century. It seemed that the station, the train, the infrastructures and the equipment had been stuck in the 1920s! Everything looked extremely old, and I sometimes imagined that I was visiting a museum of old Russia!

I wish there was no borders between states, countries and nations. These lines have deprived some people to move freely on the earth and achieve their dreams. These lines have been the cause of so many deadly wars. These lines are blamed for engaging peoples in
44

a race for race superiority. These lines have killed many talents. These lines have separated many family members. Only God knows how many people throughout history have lost their lives because of these lines! I wish I could take an eraser and clear all the lines between countries. That way no one would say, "my country," but "my earth!"

Some people are not even con10ted with barbwires and want to build great wal||ls and even make others pay for that! These are those, who in their childhood put together pieces of wood or some pillows, called them home and did not let anyone in! Now they have "grown up," but they still think like kids with a great sense of belonging! The idea of building a wall round your country and urging your neighbors to pay for it is funny. It is just like one installing a security camera for his own premise and then sends its invoice to his neighbour to pay it! The funnier thing is that they claim that building walls will keep their countries safe from terrorism; however, mass shootings and gun violence result in tens of thousands of deaths annually!

The Internet
Since 1968 when the figures about mass shooting and gun violence have been selected and collected, there have been 1,516,863 gun-related deaths on the US territories. Forget about the number of injured people!

Juho
More than one million and half people have been killed! It's horrible, but who cares?!

The Internet
Instead of *a farewell to arms*, they want to equip teachers with guns at school or appoint some police officers right in front of each school!

Juho
I've heard that. It's funny! How the students would feel? Imagine a teacher entering a class with a gun just like a sheriff!

Gun is Fun

They werrre thrrree	We werrre many
They had guns	We had pens
They had masks	We had tasks
They enterrred hurrriedly	We frrroze immediately
They orderrred furrriously	We followed desperrrately
They shouted "hey therrre	Go to amphitheaterrr"
We moved therrre	Alas! Cl.ass afterrr teacherrr
They were therrre	We werrre herrre
They starrrted acting	We werrre watching
Theirrr guns played	A bloody trrragedy
They were vertical	We were horizontal
Bodyonbody	Bloodonblood
They left alived	TV cameras arrived
The Police arrived	The ambulances arrived
Doctor after death	We had no breath
The President made speech	He he sobbed like a leech
He he made us cry	Down in tomb we lied
10 days later the leech	The President made speech
"Gun is fun"	"Wall is lull"

The Internet
Life is wide, but walls make it narrow. Walls also prevent scars from being healed! Have you read "Mending Walls" by Robert Frost?

Juho
No!

The Internet
Read it! I believe that these frontiers or walls are not only between countries but also between peoples. Their skins act as frontiers and divide them. Races are fences for some people, who still think of superiority.

Juho
True!

The train started to move, and this shattered my imagination. I lOOked out with a keen observation. I was bewildered why Russia, which is a world power, is so undeveloped! It is my understanding that those countries, which always act as the old men of the world, interfere in the internal affairs of other countries, and this would waste their time, energy, money and resources! They are always engaged in poking other countries! Consequently, they fail to cope with rapidly increasing demands of their own citizens.

Everything in its oldness was new to me! The trip opened my eyes to many facts! I learned that I should not trust whatever I hear and see in media. I learned that the distance between my eye and my ear is only 10 centimetres – too short just like the Finnish|Russian border – but that short distance makes a huge difference. I learned that seeing is believing!

In a few hours, we arrived in St. Petersburg. I had to change my train to Pushkin. However, I was starving and had to eat something. Everything had been written in Russian, and that had made the station defamiliar. I could not read even a letter! I moved around, left and right, back and forth, sometimes I just stopped and tried to find a way out. I had a feeling of a child, who had lost his mom and did not know what to do and where to go!

I approached a man, who was standing in front of a store, and asked him if he knows the exit. He just gazed at me and then said something in Russian. I didn't under.stand him at all and just left. Then, I saw a well-dressed man, reading a newspaper. Perhaps he knows English and can help me, I thought. I went toward him and asked whether he speaks English? He took his eyes from the paper, and with a hand gesture, he expressed his inability. It seemed that I could not communicate with anyone there.

After many struggles, I found my way out. I lOOked around for a few seconds and saw a restaurant on other side of the street. I hurriedly crossed the street and entered the restaurant. There were a couple of people eating there! I saw a small table in a peaceful spot just round a corner and sat there. A menu was right on the table. I opened it. It was all in Russian, and thus, I could not understand even a word of it. Soon a waitress approached me and asked something in Russian. I asked whether they have an English menu, and she said something in Russian!

Меню	
Холодные закуски	
Сельдь Олюторская	310 ₽
Таки тот "Форшмак" от Йоси	310 ₽
Трио паштетов дегустационных	310 ₽
Мясные разности	510 ₽
Килька Балтийская	310 ₽
Килька Балтийская	
Балтийские рыбы холодные, нарезанные нежно	510 ₽
Царское угощение из икры щучьей	510 ₽
Сахалинская красная икра	410 ₽
Сало разное	410 ₽
Студень с деревенской уткой	510 ₽
Икра осетровая	2010 ₽
Разности из сибирских рыб	1010 ₽

Desperately, I put my finger on one of the foods in the menu, having no idea what I had ordered. She asked me some questions in Russian, and I just nodded and smiled without knowing what I was confirming!

There were some writings on the restaurant walls, and I was curious to know what they were about, but I couldn't! I had left my language behind the border, and I felt powerless, a bit unsafe and insecure. Language has an extraordinary power. It can lessen distances between races and faces.

The waitress reappeared with a bowl in one hand and a dish in another. I was curious to see what I had ordered. She put them on the table, and I thanked her. She left with a sweet smile and came back in a few seconds with a jar of water.

I started stirring the con10ts of the bowl with a spoon. It was a red soup. I could see some pieces of beetroot and carrot in it. I tasted it carefully. Yummy! It tasted wonderful! Perhaps I can ask about its name and order it while I'm in Russia or learn about its ingredients and cook it at home, but how!? Language barrier had created a distance between us!

While eating, I scanned the behaviors of people in the street. Some women had fancy clothing, and I could detect flashy jewellery on them. Some of them who passed by the restaurant window had miniskirts and high-heeled shoes which had made them walk loudly, cautiously, lavishly and stylishly. Many of them also had soft and angular faces, light and flawless skin and slim physiques. Some women smoked cigarettes, and the smoke that they exhaled made their faces almost covered!

I finished my food and stood up to pay for it. I asked cashier how much to pay, but he could not speak English, either! I grabbed his pen, and on a piece of paper, I wrote "₽ ?" He understood what I mean, grabbed the pen from my hand and wrote "1010 ₽." I took out my wallet and paid 1100 ₽. He then returned 9x10 ₽ to me.

I then walked toward the station. I was happy that I could meet my soulmate in an hour or so, but I was not ready yet! There were several platforms, and it was a challenge for me to find the right one. With some difficulty, I scrutinized a board showing timetables in the station. Three trains departed at the same time as mine. I checked my ticket and tried to detect the same letters of the word "Pushkin" in Russian – as written on my ticket – and matched them one by one with the ones on the board to find the platform.

Juho
Пу́шкин

Juho
П

Juho
у́

Juho
ш

Juho
к

Juho
и

Juho
н

Yes, I found it: platform no. 1. I rushed to that platform and delightfully showed my ticket to a ticket inspector. He looked at it and nodded. I entered a com|part|men|t and sat, observing people through the window. Then, suddenly, I lOOked around.

Juho
Oh my gosh! Where is my hand luggage?!

My heart was in my mouth! I lOOked around again, but I could not find it. Suddenly, I remembered that I had left it in the restaurant. I looked at my watch. I had only 10 minutes to my train's departure. Immediately, I got off the train and ran at a breakneck speed toward the restaurant. I panted! What an idiot I am! How did I forget my luggage there?! What if it had been stolen?! I had never run that fast in my life. I was sure that with that speed I could break the Olympic records.

In a couple of minutes, I arrived there, but the restaurant had been closed, and its lights were off! I had a horrible feeling! I could not see inside the restaurant. I put my face directly up to the glass and tried to shield the light out with my hands around my eyes (   )

I saw a part of my hand luggage. It was still there under the table. That made me kind of relieved, but how could I get it back? Perhaps someone was still in the restaurant cleaning or washing the dishes. I peered into the restaurant, but I could not see anyone! I gently knocked on the door and waited for a short while, but no one app.eared! I looked at my watch. It was exactly the time of departure. By now, I was sure that I miss my train, and this made me extremely worried!

Juho
What would happen if I miss the train?! How can I inform Olga?

I only had her home phone number! I also had no access to internet, and if I had, she wouldn't check her emails every minute! How can I rebook my ticket while I could not speak even a Russian word! Those questions made me knock on the door as hard and as long as I could in a frenzy.

To my great surprise, the cashier appeared with sleepy eyes. As soon as he opened the door, I rushed into the restaurant, grabbed my luggage and ran out speedily toward the station. Though some minutes had passed, I was still hopeful that I will get the train, and that made me run faster.

The Book
Fabulous! Never lose hope! Move on!

My heart was jumping out of my chest. I also felt a terrible ache in my shinbones. In a few minutes, I arrived at platform 1. A train was there, but was it the same train to Pushkin?! I approached a train inspector, but I was afraid to show my ticket to him.

The Book
Do not panic! Show your ticket to him.

Juho
What if he says that my train has already gone!

The Book
Whatever happens, happens!

I showed my ticket to him. He inspected it with a pause. He then nodded. Did he mean that I have not missed the train?! I did not believe my eyes! Sometimes tardiness makes us arrive on time!

I got on the train and sat on the first seat I found empty. I wanted to faint. My whole body was wet with sweat. I was still panting: ha- ha- ha- ha- ha-

How a small mistake can affect our life! However, I was lucky to both find my hand luggage and catch the train. I felt happy. It could be worse than this!

It took me a few minutes to have a control over my body and mind. My heart was just getting back to a normal status. I took a very deeeeeeeep breath.

The train departed in 10 minutes, but no worries! Olga would learn about the delay at the Pushkin station. Perhaps delay is a part of schedule in this country!

I looked out of the window, eager for sights. The areas around the train station looked clean and modern, but the suburb looked old, shabby and dirty!

Di.vision 5
Prease & Kiss

I arrived at the Pushkin train station. I was hyper that I could see Olga again after all. I looked around and saw her waving her hand from far away. I walked toward her, and she started walking toward me, but still I didn't know how to react?! As soon as we reached each other, she opened her arms, and we hugged each other for a while. It was amazing! I really wanted this after all, and I didn't want those marvel+lous moments to end.

Olga
Welcome! Great to see you here, Juho!

Juho
Thanks!

Olga
Did you have a good trip?

Juho
Yes!

Olga
Let's go! My car is over there.

Juho
OK!

Olga
If you are hungry, we can eat something first. There is a good restaurant near here. I'm sure you'll like it, but if you are not, we can go directly to hotel.

Juho
I . . . . had a . . late lunch in . . St. Petersburg.

Olga
Alright! So let's go to your hotel and check in. You can have a short rest, and then I can come after you in an hour to start our adventure!

Juho
Good idea!

We got on her car. It was a red Lada! I cast a glance at the car exterior and interior. How Russia that produces the greatest ballistic missiles and anti-missile systems and launches space shuttles cannot produce some modern cars?!

On the way to the hotel, I had become terse again! I had nothing to say. It was as if cat had got my tongue?! What shall I say? To describe my trip, to ask some questions about her hometown, to thank her for her company, to express my extreme joy of meeting her again, or what? I had lost my self-confidence and was afraid even to open my mouth. Words have power; they can c|u|t and they can jut; they can k.ill and they can heal; they can peace and they can piss; they can bless and they can mess! Some words are like plastic bags. They are not decomposed in your h.ear.t even after 100 years.

In a few minutes, I found myself in front of a small hotel. Olga helped me fill in the hotel form, which was all in Russian, and check in. Then, she said that she will come back in an hour to walk out together and then take me for dinner to her home.

I entered my room, took out all my clothes, brushed my teeth, shaved and took a quick shower! While in shower, I decided to wash all my shyness away. I was determined to become an open, warm and friendly person. I hated being so reserved.

After the shower, I hurriedly dried my hair, used some aftershave and dressed up! When I got to the hotel lobby, she was there reading a newspaper. Upon seeing her, I was stressed out again! I stopped for a minute there and repeated my promise!

Juho
I don't want to be sheepish anymore!
I don't want to be bashful anymore!
I don't want to be terse anymore!
I want to become warm and friendly!

I took a deeeeeeeeeep breath and approached her calmly. Upon noticing me, she folded the newspaper and put it away. I stretched my hand toward her. She looked at me surprisingly! Then, she held my hand and stood up! I did not expect myself to do so! Too brave of me! But did I behave appropriately?

Juho
Olga . . . thank you for inviting me . . . to your hometown.

Olga
My pleasure!

Juho
You are very kind and of course . . . .

Olga
And of course what?
I swallowed my saliva!

Juho
Beautiful!

Olga
Oh really?! Thank you Juho!

Juho
You are, and I am very happy to . . . have you as my . . . .

Olga
As your what?

I couldn't find a proper word to complete the sen10ce. Shall I say
"friend?" But I don't want her to be merely my friend! Shall I say
"beloved," but it's too early. My mind boggled!

Juho
I mean, . . . to have you here!

Life is peace full
You're beside me
This gives me glee
***
Life is blessful
I'm behind you
Our love will never due
***
Life is peaceful
All sorrows gone
You tied your mind to mine
***

Tell me Tell me
This bless, this caress
Longs forever
Our tie dries never

We walked and talked. We told our life stories and talked about our families, interests and hobbies. We had some joint points.

At eventide, she invited me to her house. I accepted her invitation; however, I was somewhat worried about how her mom and brother would treat me. What if they don't like me and that affects Olga's perception of me? I met her mother and brother. They were kind, but unfortunately, they could not speak English, and that made our communication hard. Every now and then, Olga tried to translate some parts of our speech that she found more important. Thus, when we spoke English, they just stared at us, and when they spoke Russian, I stared at them! Language barrier brings silence, and silence brings distance!

In the meantime, I gave them their gifts. I was worried whether they would like them. They opened them immediately with a great enthusiasm and thanked me. There, I learned "thank you" in Russian: "спасибо."

After that, they set a dinner table. They had cooked some Russian cuisines for me. Different types of foods and salads had made the table colorful. I tried to taste all of them. Some were delicious, while some others tasted a bit odd. Olga tried to introduce them to me and tell me the history behind some of them, and every now and then, she was interrupted by her mom, urging her to tell me something more about the cuisines that she felt her daughter didn't know well. Consequently, Olga could not eat well.

Then, she showed their house to me. I spent some time browsing her bookshelf. She had several literary books from Alexander Pushkin, Leo Tolstoy, Anton Chekhov, Vladimir Nabokov and Fyodor Dostoyevsky. I had read some of those books.

I love|d her. I didon't want those great moments to end. I want|ed the clock to stop right t|here. She *wis* nice, pretty, caring, warm and friendly, and I always imagine|d my life with her.

I was full of her
I had a present perfect with her
But I wanted it to be present perfect continuous

At about 10 pm, her mother yawned, and I felt that I should leave. All in all, I really enjoyed meeting with them, and my impression was that our meeting had made a stronger tie of intimacy among all of us. Olga did drive me back to the hotel. On the way, I lis10ed to her at10tively and could not take my eyes off her. I knew that I couldn't see her until tomorrow!

Olga
What time shall we meet tomorrow?

Juho
Any time you wish!

Olga
Let's meet at 10 am in front of the hotel, right?

Juho
Great! спасибо!

Olga
My pleasure!

Soon we arrived at the hotel. I wanted to cuddle and kiss her passionately, but what if this causes a misunderstanding for her! That might ruin my trip and could affect our newly-built relationship!

Juho
See you tomorrow!

Olga
See you. Good night!

We don't know how far we can go in a newly-built relationship; any relationship! Sometimes we move fast, but our partner is not ready yet, and this causes some misunderstandings! Sometimes and based on an experience, we cautiously move at a slow pace, while our partner wants it to be faster, and this creates a distance. S|he might think that if s|he expresses her|his tendency, that might damage the relationship, and in some cases, s|he expects us to understand what s|he demands! What if we could clearly say what we wish for in a relationship, and how deep we wish to dig in! This way everyone will understand what we desire, and they let us know whether we are on the right track! This way we do not waste our time and energy in a relationship. Otherwise, if we expect others to understand what we really desire with some indirect signs, we never get at what we really wish!

I went to bed, but I could not sleep. All I had seen and all she had said passed quickly from my mind. I had no idea how to push our relationship forward a bit further and how to win her heart for good. Shall I become direct? But how would she react if I become direct? Will I ruin everything, or will I get whatever I expect? I had no idea! Indeterminacy kills!

Juho
Good morning, Olga!

Olga
Good morning! Did you have a good night sleep?

Juho
Yes!

Why did I tell lies? I couldn't get a wink of sleep! What if I could say, "No, not really! I could not sleep at all, because I was thinking of you all night!"

Olga
Good to hear that! Let's continue our exploration!

It was sunny. We visited Alexander Park, a cathedral and a couple of museums. On the way, she introduced her hometown and the history behind it with pride and joy, and I lis10ed at10tively. Then, we had lunch in one of her favorite restaurants. In the restaurant, we also had a very ex10sive discussion about any subject that came up. I really enjoyed lis10ing to her. We had a nice day to-gether. I learned a lot about Russia, its culture, climate, history and people, especially in Pushkin! By the end of the day, she drove me back to the hotel, and we set a time together to meet again tomorrow.

She was full of beans, which charged my flat battery; however, I had not managed to get rid of my reserved sentiment and sheepishness that had always prevented me from saying right words at right times and doing right things at right moments! I had not been totally defrosted yet even after spending two days with her. There happened occasions that she passed the ball to me, providing the ground for me to score a goal, but I missed the goal! I could win her heart for good with some compliments, which cost but nothing, but I failed! I had only a day to go, and I had to hit the bullseye with my darts; otherwise, I would be a loser!

I had another sleepless night! In the morning, I took a shower, watched some news in Russian, had my breakfast, walked for a few minutes around the hotel and took some photos until she showed up! Upon seeing her, I went toward her and wanted to cuddle her, but I failed. Ah! How long is it going to continue? We continued our tour. Abruptly, I stopped and gazed at her for a while.

Olga
What's wrong!?

Juho
Nothing!

Olga
So why do you stare at me like that!?

Juho
Because . . . *you* . . . look . . .

Olga
I look what?

Juho
. . . . pretty!

Olga
Really!?

Juho
Yes! You . . . look like an angel, baby!

Olga
спасибо!

Silence reigned for a while!

Olga Juho

How does she feel now?! Does silence mean glee? Does silence mean gloom?

In the evening, I suggested going to a bar, and she agreed! It was too crowded, and we found a small table somewhere in the middle! We ordered some alcoholic beverages and tried to communicate, but the pitch of noise was so high that we could not hear each other.

Olga
ॠ ॳ ॳ Ƌ ॳ Ж ЧЇ ৳?

Juho
What?!
64

We had to speak loudly and word by word!

Olga
I . . . said . . . morrow . . . you . . . are . . . leaving!

Juho
Right!

Olga
I . . . wish . . . you . . . could . . . stay . . . longer!

I was surprised to hear that. Is she into me?

Juho
Ya, . . . I wish . . . I . . . could, but . . .

Olga
But what?

Juho
But my . . . job does not . . . let me. I hope . . . to . . . come back . .
soon.

Olga
Would . . . be . . . great!

Juho
But . . . I . . . miss . . . you!

Olga
I . . . miss . . . you . . . too!

Juho
Really?!

Olga
Yes!

Juho
Would . . . you . . . like to . . . . dance?

Olga
Ya! There . . . is a . . . nice . . . nightclub . . . next door. Shall . . we . . . go . . . there?

Juho
Of course!

I held her hand and walked toward that nightclub. We paid the entrance fee and started dancing. This reminded me of our dance on the Silja Symphony! Since then, a great progress in our relationship had happened, but that was not sufficient. I wanted more!

My sweetheart danced well. I could not take my eyes off her even for a second. The dance lighting had made her face colorful and more attractive. Her moves moved me! I moved my head closer to hers and rested it on her shoulder for a while. Then, I looked at her again, who was dancing joyfully and to the rhythm. I tried to adapt my moves with hers. Suddenly, I lost it and moved my lips toward hers. She showed no reluctance, and I started kissing her passionately. I was acting like a starving per.son, licking her lips noisily! I did not believe it was *me* doing so! It was incredible! How would it be possible?! I suppose vodka had shot my sheepishness and made me so brave.

For a second, I opened my eyes, but after I saw her closed eyes, I shut my eyes again. We had stopped dancing and we were just kissing noisily, which was not heard at all amongst the high-pitched noises. My dream was coming true, but it had not come yet! I felt I was the happiest person on the whole entire globe!

Olga
Shall we sit down?

Juho
OK!

We sat down, but I still wanted to kiss her. I moved my chair closer to her, put my hand around her waist and started kissing her again. Then, on the spur of the moment, she stood up and started styling her hair with her right hand.

Olga
Shall we leave, Juho?

Juho
As you wish!

We left the club and moved toward the hotel. That was the last night I was in Pushkin, and I wished to spend the whole night with her. Shall I invite her to my room? What if she says "NO!"

Juho
It was great to be with you today!

Olga
Pleased to hear that!

Juho
I don't want this night to end!

Olga
Olga

Her silence made me hesitant to invite her in directly! Silence has many different significations: satisfaction, reluctance, patience, hesitancy, depression, anger, envy, etc.

We arrived at the hotel. I kissed her once again in the car as long as I could, and she showed no resistance! This encouraged me to invite her to my room.

Juho
Would you like to come in?

Olga
You know . . . if I go home late, my mom gets worried!

Juho
I see!

Olga
See you tomorrow at 10. I'll take you to the station.

Juho
Thanks! Good night!

Di.vision 6
Pierce & Fierce

Early in the morning, I got up and packed up. I was upset that I was leaving! I had just been able to plant a seed of love in her heart, and distance might not let it grow, but I had no choice! She picked me up at 10 and headed for the train station. On the way, we were both silent.

Olga Juho
Olga Juho
Olga Juho

Silence here signified desolation. Our silence could reveal that we were into each other. She parked her car and accompanied me to platforms. She cast a look at my ticket and directed me to platform no. 1. The train had not arrived yet. She was staring at me with her gloomy eyes, but when I looked at her, she looked away quickly. This made me gaze at her for a while and scan every inch of her face, every strand of her hair and every cell of her skin. She was full of grace and beauty. She was the one whom I wished for. It was as if God had designed and moulded her just for me. To my surprise, tears stung her eyes, but immediately, she turned away. Her tears, however, made me happy, since they could prove her true love! I approached her, kissed her forehead and wiped her tears from her cheeks with my forefinger. I swallowed a lump in my throat, but I tried to look b.old. I cleared my voice:

Juho
Olga, you are . . . kind, caring and . . . pretty, and I . . . love you!

Olga
Miff . . . I love you, too!

I was pleased to hear that! I hugged her as hard as I could and then started kissing her. Her lips tasted salty, but it was sweeter than the Fazer chocolate to me!

OlgaJuho
OlgaJuho
OlgaJuho

My train arrived, but I wished it had never arrived. I wanted to stay with her in Russia forever.

Juho
Olga, let's keep in touch!

Olga
Sure!

Juho
See you soon again, either here or there.

Olga
Yes, take care!

I touched and caressed her soft hair, kissed her cheek and got on the train. I took a seat next to the window and gazed at her until the train left the station and left my heart right there. In chocked desolation, I lOOked back and waved my hand as much as I could, and she waved back. In less than 10 seconds, I could not see her anymore!

70

On the way back home, I just felt like someone dizzy. My eyes could see but nothing! My appetite had shrunk. I just imagined our future together. I could not get her off my mind even for a tick, and my mind replayed all her words and deeds repeatedly.

Eventually, I arrived|alived home tired! I did not attend my workplace for a couple of days, pre10ding that I was sick! Indeed, I was sick. I was deep in love, and love is a disease. I didn't want to talk to or meet with anybody. I preferred seclusion. A couple of times, my phone rang, but I did not care. In the meantime, I sent Olga an email, thanking her of her hospitability and informing her of my arrival. She replied soon, and her answer cherished high hopes in me.

After a couple of days, I called her a couple of times, but no one answered the phone. I was kind of worried. Where is she? What is she doing? I called her again, but no answer! I called her several times, and her mother finally answered the phone. As soon as she heard my name, she called out to her daughter.

Olga
Hello Juho!

Juho
Hei honey! How are you?

Olga
I'm fine, but . . . I miss you here!

Juho
I miss you, too! I wish I was there or you were here!

Olga
So do come over again!

Juho
Sure, as soon as I can!

Olga
I have an exam tomorrow. Keep your fingers crossed for me!

Juho
I'll do! You are clever, and you will pass with flying colors!

Olga
Thanks!

Juho
So go and study. Talk to you later. Good night!

Olga
OK. Good night!

A few months flew by. I either called her or exchanged some emails with her. I sent her some photos of Tampere and my workplace. I then invited her to visit Finland, and she tacitly accepted my invitation. I was on cloud nine! I quickly made a preliminary plan for her visit in my mind: to visit Helsinki together for a couple of days and then visit Tampere. I made a list of touristy attractions in Helsinki and Tampere and did some research on the history beyond those places. Then, I sent her an email, notified her of my plans and asked for her opinion. She did not reply my email for about 10 days. It was kind of weird. I called her several times, but no one answered the phone. What has happened to her?! This made me call her several times, but no reply!

Juho
Juho

After a while, she sent me an email, saying that unfortunately she cannot visit me! What was wrong? Why did she change her mind? What made her change her mind? Have I done something wrong? Has her mom disagreed? I read and reread my emails several times and pondered on my words used in my phone calls to see if I had done or said something inappropriate. I could not detect anything! So what was wrong? Was she still in love with me? Has she changed her mind? Out of sight, out of mind?!

I knew that if this went on for a while, I would lose her! What could I do? I decided to visit her again and water the seed that once I had planted in her heart. I called her again and again, and eventually, she answered the phone. I happily notified her of my plan to visit her and asked her for an invitation letter and a hotel booking confirmation. I imagined that this would surprise her, but she shocked me!

Juho
Why don't you want me to visit you?!

Olga
This is not a proper time!

Juho
Tell me what's the matter?

Olga

I'm extremely busy, and I cannot serve you as I should!

Juho

I just want to have a reunion with you and nothing more! I don't expect you to . . .

Olga

I said that this is not a proper time!

My curiosity was k.illing me. I knew there was something wrong, and she attempted not to disclose it. That made me more disturbed. Perhaps she had become remorseful and wanted to break up with me. My curiosity made me more demanding! At first, she refused to take the lid off, but my constant insistence and persistence broke her resistance. There was an ocean of grief in her voice! That made me both upset and worried!

Olga

You know . . . a . . . couple . . . of months ago,

She suddenly burst out crying and cried her heart out! This lacerated my soul. I was speechless!

Olga

Boo ````````` Hoo ````````` Miff````````` Booo´´´´´´´´´

Juho

Don't cry! What's happened?!

Olga

Booo ````````` Hooo ````````` Miff ````````` Boo ´´´´´´´´´ Mif one of my . . . classmates . . . invited me to . . . . . his place to . . . study . . . together for our . . . exam.

74

Her voice was quivering!

Juho
Aha?!

Olga
Olga

Olga
I . . . trusted him . . . and . . .

Juho
And what?

Olga
And . . . vi.sited his . . . place.

Juho
What happened then?

An agonizing sob suddenly tore from her throat! The sob con-
stricted her throat, cutting off words she couldn't bring herself to
say anyway. She tried to swallow her sob and continue her story.
It took a while.

Olga
In the meantime, we . . . ate and drank . . . together.

Juho
Aha . . . .

Olga
And when I got drunk . . . he . . . . raped . . . me!

Juho
Oh no!

Olga

I stopped . . . my . . friendship . . . with him and tried . . . to . . hide it, but . . now . . . .

Juho

Now what?

Juho	Olga
Olga	Juho
Juho	Olga

Olga

Now I've . . . found . . . that . . . I'm . . . . pregnant!

I died

He was gazing at me strangely
I looked down, feeling badly
He appro.ached meee
I went back with plea
He was not he
I had to flee
He had lost it
I had no key
"No!" I said
He not cared
He clasped me & paid no heed
He had a very grave greed
He came fore
Put me on floor
My heart pressed hard
I had no guard
He was fat
I was flat
His tool tore me
He was carefree
I had pain
He was Cain

I sobbed
He jobbed
He was done
And had fun
"Sorry" he said
I bled & bled & bled
"Sorry it lasted short"
I had to abort!

She burst out crying again! Hearing her sobs moved me dramatically. My temp suddenly rose, and I started sweating. I could not believe my ears! I wanted to fly to Russia, find that bastard and chew his throat!

Juho
What the heck! Did you report this to police?

Olga
Miff . . . . No!

Juho
Have you informed your mom?

Olga
Not yet!

Juho
You should!

She started crying again, and that made me totally cross!

Olga
After learning about . . . my pregnancy, he is . . . . . . scared to death . . . and urges me to . . . abort the baby, but I'm afraid . . . to do so!

Juho
So what are you going to do?!

Olga
He says that . . . he loves me and . . . .

Juho
And what?

Olga
and wants to marry me!

I went speechless! The whole of me burned down all of a sudden,

but still I tried to find myself back.

Juho
Are you sure he loves you?

Olga
He says so!

Juho
But I love you, too!

Olga
I know, but . . . but what else can I do now? I don't want to abort
my baby, and I . . . have only one choice: to marry him!

Juho
Oh no! It's not a *choice*; it is a *force*!

Olga
I have a request.

Juho
What's that?

Olga
Do you promise to do it for me?

Juho
Of course!

Olga
Please *forget* about me.

Juho
What do you mean?

Olga
I know you love me but forget about me.

Juho
But

Olga
But me no buts!

Juho
But Olga you are making up for a petty mistake with a mortal one!
Olga
Maybe, but I've made up my mind!

I wished I was dead! I dropped the receiver and fainted - - - - - - -

Di.vision 7
Peace & Geese

I became de.pressed! I felt like a businessperson who had lost all his capitals, properties and savings in one single moment! I was emotionally broke! Life had become meaningless to me, and I had no motivation to live.

I was always in bed, either closing my eyes or staring at ceiling! Because of inactivity, I suffered from a terrible backache. Perhaps she was not honest with me or perhaps she made up that story to get rid of me! Perhaps she had been in a serious relationship with that per.son for a while, and after this happened to her, she had no choice but to reveal her secret! How I fell in love with someone with one single look, and why I trusted someone whom I knew nothing of her background? These thoughts made my blood boil!

I was full of despair. For a while, I did not at10d my workplace. One night, I heard my phone ring. I did not answer it! It rang and rang and rang until my head off! I dragged myself out of bed and answered the phone. It was my boss! He wanted to talk to me in person! It was clear like a day that he was cross with me. Perhaps he wanted to fire me! Nothing mattered anymore!

Next day, I visited his office. I could detect displeasure in his face.

The Boss
What's wrong with you, Juho?

Juho

Nothing!

The Boss

Nothing?! What do you mean nothing?! You have not at10ded your workplace for about 10 days without per.mission and say NOTHING! Tell me what's wrong. Perhaps I find a way for it. Our customers have sent me complaint letters, saying that you do not answer their inquiries. They have made some orders, but they have not received them yet after long! This cannot continue!

Juho

So fire me and hire another person.

The Boss

True, but when I remember your sense of commitment in the olden days, I change my mind. You are the same hardworking person, but I don't know what has happened to you!

Juho

You are right! There is something wrong with me!

The Boss

What's it, Juho? Tell me!

Juho

I badly fell in love and broke the bone of my *mind*!

The Boss

What do you mean?!

Juho

I mean, I loved a Russian girl, but then she was abducted and raped, and now she is pregnant!

The Boss

Take it easy, Juho! Don't let such trivial issues ruin your days! The world is full of beautiful girls. Once a friend of mine fell in love with a girl, but that girl didn't love him. He committed suicide, but after he was transferred to a hospital, he immediately fell in love with a nurse who was taking care of him and totally forgot about his ex-beloved!

He burst out laughing!

The Boss
Find another one, this time from Thailand. Look at me! I have already married four times, but I am still in a *standby* mode, and I don't want to stop here.

Juho
Juho
Juho

The Boss
Go ahead, explore the world, try different ones and see which one is sweeter. Women are like fruits. Eat and enjoy them, and don't limit yourself to one single fruit. It becomes boring!

Juho
Juho

The Boss
Now I ask Sirkku to take care of your duties. You are totally flat now! Go and pump yourself up and come back on Monday.

Immediately, I left there and decided to go to a restaurant. On the way, I pondered on my boss's words. How can I do so? In the restaurant, I ordered my favorite food and browsed through a newspaper. My favorite music was on, but my horrible mood had changed it to a piss of musick to my ear. I had no appetite and left the food half-eaten.

After the lunch, I walked to a park wherein some geese, ducks, goats, swans and chickens were kept. I had heard that spending some time with animals would help people, suffering from depression, alleviate their mental problems and distresses! I fed the goats, and their rivalry to take tree branches from my hand were delightful, but remembering how that bastard got the branch out of my mouth made me hot under the collar again!

The Old Woman
They are amazing! Every day I walk here to watch them!

Juho
Really?!

The Old Woman
Yes, they remind me of my sons. When they were young, they had two goats just like them. Sweet olden days!

Juho
Where are your sons now?!

The Old Woman
They moved to the US!

Juho
How often do you see them?

The Old Woman
How often? I saw them around 10 years ago.

Juho
10 years ago?!

The Old Woman
Yes!

Juho
Too looooooooooong!

The Old Woman
It seems that they have forgotten that they have a mom here! They are both married and have some kids, but I am sure they soon become old, and their kids leave them unat10ded as they left me!

Her words moved me! I just remembered that I have not visited my own mom for long, either. I returned home, called my mom and informed her that I am visiting her during weekend. She was extremely delighted.

Soon I packed up and went to the train station, and in a couple of hours I found myself in the bOsOm of my mom. I felt like a newly-born baby. Visiting my mom helped me ease my 10sions! It was a nice reunion! My mom had a lot to say, and I just lis10ed at10tively to her! I just wanted her to talk!

I went to bed late that night, but I had a good night sleep after all! After the breakfast, my mom and I first visited a cemetery wherein my dad was buried. She said that she frequently visited there, planted some flowers or watered them. Spending 10 minutes on my dad's grave sufficed that I quickly review all my past family life and my parents' affection! Tears rolled down my cheeks uncontrollably and made me kind of relieved!

Next, my mom and I went to a swimming pool, which I used to use when I was living there. I remembered my childhood friends, but they have now spread throughout the whole world! Everyone everywhere! I asked my mom about some of them. She knew what had happened to a few of them, since their families were still residing in that town; however, some had migrated from that town along with their families, and my mom had no idea what had happened to them!

I got undressed! A piece of mirror|rorrim did catch my eyes! I took a step forward and gazed at my own body for a while! It was just an empty body with no spirit! I had to inject some spirit into it! I left the changing room, took a quick shower and walked toward the pool where my mom was waiting just for me. I remembered the olden days when I was a kid, full of zest for life. I did not understand what love is, but I loved everything wholeheartedly: birds, bears, rats, cats, trees, bees, lakes, snakes, mom and dad. When we went to a lake in our neighbourhood, my mom was always there for me with a towel in hand to dry me.

I took a deep breath and immersed in water for 10 seconds. It helped me drown all my griefs in water, feel light, float on water!

I had a great time with my mom. On Sunday afternoon, I left there. My mom who could not take her eyes off me accompanied me to the train station. The closer we got to the station, the more desolate she looked.

The Mom
Visit me more often, son!

Juho
I'll do!
86

The Mom
I have only you in this world! Visit me!

Juho
Sure!

The Mom
Call me after you arrive home!

Juho
Of course!

The Mom
Safe trip!

I hugged her as hard as I could! A huge hug! While hugging my mom, I felt I was the happiest per.son on the earth, since right at that moment, some people were putting the coffins of their parents in grave, or in a hospital just a kilometre away from the station, some people were lying dying and were taking their last breath!

Di.vision 8
Park & Spark

I visited the office on Monday as fresh as a daisy. I had returned to my normal life. The Boss and some of my colleagues had made some coffee and cake, and we all got together during our coffee break. I needed this after all! That was the last shot to the body of my depression! How people around us can make us feel good, and vice versa! I decided to be the one who makes others feel good.

The Boss
Welcome back, Juho! We are happy to have you back here!

Sirkku
Yes, we are happy to see you again after all!

Juho
Thank you all! I am proud to have you as my colleagues and friends here!

The Boss
Juho, don't forget to eat different fruits. Body needs different vitamins and not one single one! Do you understand what I mean?

Juho
Juho
Juho

The Boss
Now let us get back to business!

My life had returned to its normal trend. I had stuck a note on my fridge door.

Call my mom
Work hard
Smile ☺
Do exercises
Hang out with friends
Eat & sleep well
Help anyone who might need me
Sleep enough
Read books

Whenever I went to the kitchen, I noticed that note and checked whether I had done them in this week?

Juho
Have I called my mom in this week? Oh, no! Let me do it right now!

Juho
Hi mom! How are you?

The Mom
Fine! Thanks for calling!

Juho
What's your plan for this weekend?

The Mom
No particular plan yet!

Juho
So come to Tampere. We can spend some time together.

The Mom
Really?!

Juho
Yes, why not?

The Mom
OK. I'll come!

Juho
Great. See you soon.

For a while, I used to visit the park wherein I had met The Old Woman. She made me care more about my mom, and I wanted to find her and pay it back to her. Let me say that I always believe that we should not just pay it back; we should pay it forward as well. This helps us to spread kindness. Perhaps I could help her get out of solitude. I failed to find her. Is she sound? If so, why doesn't she visit the park? How can I find her? I had no clue!

I did buy a bunch of flowers and went to the station on Saturday noontime. Flowers should be gifted to the living people, but we usually give them to late ones! Visit a cemetery near your house, and you will think it's a flower garden, but how many of these flowers are gifted to the living people?!

My mom arrived. I hugged her again as if I had not seen her for 10 years! We had a brunch in a restaurant and then visited a shopping mall. We did some shopping and had some ice-creams. Right after that, we walked home together.

Upon entering my flat, my mom started to clean up, cook, iron my shirts, wash my pillow covers and blankets - - - - - - - - - -

Juho
Mom, you have not come over to clean up. You have come here to relax.

The Mom
No problem son!

Juho
Thank you!

ᘖᘖᘖᘖᘖᘖᘖᘖᘖᘖ

Mom hosts me for nine months with care in her womb

She loves me unconditionally until she enters the tomb

ᘖᘖᘖᘖᘖᘖᘖᘖᘖᘖ

On Sunday morning, I decided to take my mom to the park and show those animals to her. When we arrived, I noticed an old woman sitting there on a bench. Is she The Old Woman? I was not sure. I fixed my gaze on her and walked toward her speedily_____ My mom was left behind.

Yes, she was The Old Woman! I approached her excitedly.

Juho
Hello! Do you remember me?

She stared at me for a few seconds.

The Old Woman
Of course!

I pointed to my mom, who was still a few steps behind me.

Juho
This is my mom!

The Old Woman
Nice!

By this time, my mom had joined us.

Juho
Mom, this is . . .

The Old Woman
Satu!

She stood up, stretched her hand and shook hands with my hand!

The Mom
I'm Leena! Nice to meet you!

Satu
Nice to meet you, too!

We sat on the same bench.

Juho
I visited the park almost every day to meet you again, but I . . . .

Satu
Really!? I got flu and had to stay at home!

The Mom
How do you feel now?

Satu
Much better!

Juho
Mom, I met Satu here some time ago. She has two sons, who now live in the US. Her story that her sons have not visited her for about 10 years touched me and made me think that I should visit you more often.

Satu
Oh, Really!?

Juho
Yes!

The Mom
Thank you, Satu!

Juho
I have an idea! Let's spend the day together.

Satu looked at me in awe for a few seconds and nodded with a smile. We left the park, walked for a while and then decided to have lunch in a restaurant. We had a long discussion about many different things. Satu narrated her impressive life story to us. While lis10ing to her, a spark ignited in my head. I shall write her narratives down! These people are a reservoir of narratives, of history and of experience. They should be written. They should be read. They should be heard. I notified Satu of my decision to write her stories down, and she was con10t. She wrote down her home address and phone number on a piece of paper and gave it to me. That reminded me of the moment when Olga gave me her email address!

Destiny is the best author I know. S|he deserves the Nobel Prize for Literature. I am always shocked how the hand of destiny uses its skills to create lots of rising actions, climaxes, falling actions, suspense and resolutions in our life, and sometimes even before we experience a resolution, it destines another set of rising actions, climaxes, falling actions and suspense for us. Many vicissitudes we experience in our life, and that makes our life dynamic!

After the lunch, we went to a nearby forest and hunted some mushrooms and berries. We had fun together. Satu and my mom looked happy, and I was happy that I could gratify them. Sometimes we can inject happiness in the hearts and minds of others for little or no cost, and that positive energy comes back to us.

I had a great time with my mom in Tampere. On Monday morning, I took her to the train station, and she left. As soon as she left, I missed her! Parents are treasures, but we find them late in our life, and sometimes we do not see their real value plus 24% of value added tax! During our childhood, we think of them as heroes. Our dad seems to be a *Deus ex Machina*, who can make impossible possible; however, during our teenage, they lose their credits in our eyes. They look old-fashioned! They think old as if they belong to the Medieval Times! We enjoy hanging out with our friends and follow what our friends say or do! This distance and conflict of interests go on until we pass three to four decades of our life, and then we *might* start loving them anew if they are still alive. What a lengthy circle!

Di.vision 9
Phone & Own

While I was browsing the library shelves to find some books, by mere chance, I came across a book about Russia. This reminded me of Olga. I was eager to know what she is doing, but I had no connection or relation with her. 10 months had passed since our last phone call. Perhaps she has delivered her baby by now. Is that a s|he? How does s|he look like? What is her|his name? Alternatively, perhaps she has eventually aborted it. Are they still together? Do they have a warm life? Do they feel happy? Anyway, that did not matter to me anymore. Though I had lost her in the unfair game of life, I always wished them a happy life!

One night, I came home tired. I had received several orders from several customers in Russia and had to handle them as soon as I could. On the way, I ordered a pizza, and as soon as I arrived home, I went directly to the kitchen and started eating it. I had not taken the first slice that I heard my phone ring! Who's that? Perhaps that's my mom. *She* usually calls at this time!

With that slice of pizza in my mouth, I went toward the phone and looked at its ID caller. It was an unknown number! Who is s|he?

Juho
Juho Siltamäki!

Olga
Hello Juho!

Juho
Hello! Who are you?!

Olga
It's me, Olga!

Juho
Olga?!

Juho
Juho
Juho

I went speechless! I had a mixed feeling. I didn't know whether to feel happy or sad. I was happy, since she was there on the phone, talking to me, and sad, since I thought she would create another climax in my life and shatter my peace of mind!

Olga
Yes. Have you forgotten me?!

Juho
No way, but I'm sort of . . . astonished! I didn't expect you to . . . call me!

Olga
I see.

Juho
How are you . . . doing?

Olga
Just getting back to a normal life!

Juho
What . . . do you mean?!

Olga
My story is too long and might need a *noveramatry*!

Juho
No problem! I'm all . . . ears!

She was hesitant to start!

Olga
Olga

Juho
Go ahead!

Olga
I really don't know how to start, but let me first say that I'm a mom now.

Juho
Really?! Congrats!

Olga
Thanks!

Juho
Is that a he or a she?

Olga
A boy!

Juho
What's his name?

Olga
Vladimir.

Juho
A pure Russian name, isn't it?

Olga
Yes!

Juho
What's your . . . spouse doing?

Olga
My spouse?!

Juho
Yes!

Olga
That . . . guy . . . abandoned me . . a few months before . . . Vladimir is born!

Juho
A.ban.doned you!?

Olga
Yes, he abandoned me and left Pushkin!

Juho
Bastard! He putt butt and . . . . how could he do that?

Olga
I don't know! He just left me, and no one knows . . . where on earth he is now!

Juho
These mongrels . . . ruin the lives of . . . others for their own instant pleasure!

Olga
Right! I was [de]pressed for a while, but now . . . I'm just going back to a normal life!

Juho
Fine!

Olga
How about you? . . . Is everything fine!

I sighed!

Juho
Let's say fine!?

Olga
What do you mean?!

Juho
Um, just like you . . . I've just recovered . . . from a treble . . . [de]pression!

Olga
No way! What for?

Juho
For . . . your . . . love!

Olga	**Juho**
Olga	**Juho**
Olga	**Juho**

Olga
Sorry to hear that!

Juho
We were both . . . victimized, but let bygones . . . . be bygones!

Olga
True! What are you doing now? Are you in a relationship?

Juho
No!

Olga
Really!?

Juho
Yes!

Olga
Olga
Olga

Olga
To be honest with you, I've called to say that . . . I'm . . .

Juho	**Olga**
Olga	**Juho**
Juho	**Olga**

Juho
You are what? Pregnant again?!

She laughed out loud in a frenzy!

Olga
No! I'm interested to visit you!

I could not believe my ears!

Juho
Really?!

Olga
Yes!

Her love pumped itself up anew in my heart and mind. All of a sudden, all dark clouds of gloom disappeared from my mind, and the sky of my mind became serene as if I had woken up from a nightmare. I was happy that the hand of destiny was giving her back to me after all!

Olga
It's for about 11 days that I'm gonna call you, but in fact, I wasn't sure if you were receptive!

Juho
Why not?!

Olga
I ruined your life.

Juho
As I said, we both were victims, weren't we? I only blame that . . guy, who dried our love . . . for the sake of his own desire! So let me know . . . when you are visiting me!

Olga
Sure! See you soon.

As soon as I hanged off, I started walking fast from side to side of my flat! How would it be possible? I still could not believe this has happened in reality. What is her in10tion of visiting me? I was shocked! My mind became busy again. I forgot my hunger, dressed up again and went out walking! I walked and walked and walked with no particular destination and talked and talked and talked to myself loudly in streets!

I came back home. It was 11 pm. I brushed my teeth, but then I not.iced the pizza on the table. I gobbled up the rest of my pizza. It was stale and cold, but I still enjoyed it. Then, I brushed my teeth again and went to bed. I could not sleep! As soon as I closed my eyes, she appeared, and I reviewed every single moment from the time I first saw her on the Silja Line dance stage until a few hours ago that we talked on the phone. I wanted her badly right now! I felt like a dry tree that blossoms once again in spring!

The springtime of my life had started. I was so hyper to see her soon here in Finland, and I had to do whatever I could to make a lovely and memorable stay for her.e! I remembered my former plan. We stay a few days in Helsinki and then spend a few days in Tampere.

After a few days, she called me and notified me of the time that suits her the most for her trip. She had decided to visit me after her final exams. I could see her in a few months. During this time, I was in contact with her by either phone or email and sent her the required documents for her visa application. She sent me a few photos of Vladimir by email, and I sent her some of my mom's photos. In the meantime, I visited Satu every now and then and lis10ed to her narratives, while jotting down some keywords, which helped me write her story down in detail. I was confident that her story would be interesting for some people, who are fond of historical fiction and|or fictional history.

Di.vision 10

Pass & Path

Vladimir and I received our visas and got on a train from Pushkin to St. Petersburg. I was excited to see Juho after all. He seemed to be a kind, protective and trustworthy man. I hope I do not make another mistake. My trust to my classmate changed the direction of my life, left a scar on my soul, ruined my personal life and left me in despair. I remembered the occasions that I was at the edge of committing suicide, but I'm happy that I did not do so. We shall not resolve a petty mistake with another fatal mistake. Now I have to do whatever I can to raise Vladimir and make a bright future for him.

Soon we were at the St. Petersburg station, and we had to change our train. Due to my frequent trips to St. Petersburg, I know its station like the back of my hand. However, it was demanding to travel with Vladimir and a luggage. That was my first experience of traveling with him, but I had to get used to it. He is a part of me hereafter, and I should learn how to handle everything by myself.

We got on a train from St. Petersburg to Finland border. Vladimir fell asleep, and this gave me some time to eat some sandwiches I had made. I looked out of the window and stretched my hands several times to lessen the pain in them, but how could I lessen the pain of my bad memories? Perhaps I need to stretch my mind, too!

I decided not to travel back in the dark tunnels of my life but to travel forward in the bright highways with high hopes. There will be many marvellous adventures for my son and me.

I was happy to see Finland once again. I had once visited Helsinki and loved it. Hell sinks in Helsinki! It looked like a safe and modern city, but how Tampere would look like? Anyway, does Juho love me after all? Does what my classmate did to me affect his affection to me? How does he react when he sees Vladimir? Does my son decrease his love to me? Will I have a good time in Finland? I had lots of questions, and only the pass.age of time could answer them. Soon Vladimir woke up crying, and his tears tore my thoughts apart. I breastfed him, and soon he fell asleep in my bOsOm again. Now I understand what my mom had done for me, and her concerns are not over yet!

We arrived to the border. We got off the train and passed the security gates and official checkpoints of Russia and then of Finland. Our passports were stamped twice first at the Russian checkpoint at the time of departure and then at the Finnish checkpoint upon entry. It was a long and tiresome process. As soon as I got on a train to Helsinki, I felt relieved! I took a deep breath and closed my eyes.

As soon as the train left the station, I opened my eyes and looked out meticulously. I could clearly detect some differences between here and there at first sight. These were the differences that I had not.iced in my last visit to Finland, too. The train looked more
106

modern, cleaner, faster and smoother with more facilities. The highways and roads that the train crossed looked clean and modern. We seem to be a bigger, stronger and more influential country in the world equations, but why Finland looks finntastic?!

Before we arrive at the Helsinki main train station, I left Vladimir, who was asleep like a log, on a seat, went to the train toilet and quickly brushed my teeth. I was worried that he might wake up and fall off the seat. Then, I hurriedly combed my hair and used some makeup. Some makeup artists believe that a good moisturizer is enough. However, I like to use a makeup primer before my foundation for a radiant and natural finish. Then, I browsed my dress in the mirror. I had put on a modest black white and gray check patterns all over, which I believed was of good omen to me! I had a couple of chic expensive dresses that I believed were of bad omen in my life, so every time I put them on, something bad would happen to me and piss my days off! Thus, those dresses look brand new after several years!

I opened the toilet's door. A fat man was behind the door roaring! He looked daggers at me. It seemed that he had been waiting for long, and his kidneys and bowels were bursting!

Hurriedly, I went toward Vladimir. Thankfully, he was still asleep. I wore some perfume. The train announcement in three different languages, announcing that we are approaching the Helsinki main train station made Vladimir wake up. I styled his blond hair with my hand and tried to clean his face with a wet tissue. I didn't want Juho to see him in a sleepy mode!

Soon we got off the train. I could see Juho waving hands and walking speedily toward us; however, my luggage did not allow me to move speedily toward him. As soon as he reached me, he softly hugged Vladimir and me together. For a few seconds, we all had become one hybrid body.

Juho
Welcome! Happy to see you again!

Olga
Thanks! Mutual feeling!

Juho
Wow! Look at him! He is cute!

Olga
Happy to hear that!

He then stretched his hands and held Vladimir in his arms. Juho looked super excited! I had a good feeling that Juho was very receptive to my son.

Soon after, we moved toward a parking place where Juho had parked his car. Juho held Vladimir, while I dragged the luggage behind myself. After a few minutes, we found ourselves behind a new white modern Chevrolet. Juho had even installed a baby seat in his car for Vladimir! It was amazing! Juho drove directly toward a hotel that he had booked for us. He helped us check in and carried our luggage into our room.

Juho
Have a short rest and then come to the hotel lobby. I'll be waiting for you there in an hour, OK?

Olga
Why waiting in the hotel lobby for us?

Juho
So where shall I wait?

Olga
Here!

Juho
Really?

Olga
Of course! Come on in, come on in!

He grinned from ear to ear, entered the room and sat on a sofa. After changing Vladimir's diaper and feeding him, Juho started playing with him. He made some funny faces and sounds, and Vladimir laughed loudly. He then moved a toy over his head, and Vladimir tried to grab it with his hands. It was as if Juho was Vladimir's real father.

Juho
How were your exams?

Olga
I really don't know!

Juho
You'll pass them with flying colors!

Olga
I don't think so!

Juho
Why?!

Olga
Vladimir needs lots of at10tion, and I couldn't study well.

Juho
I see! By the way, you . . . smell . . . really . . . good!

Olga
Thank you!

I was really pleased to hear that! I took out my perfume from my handbag and showed it to Juho.

Olga
I usually wear this one.

Juho stood up and approached me to see the name of the perfume!

Juho
Crazy Lady!? But you are not *crazy*!

Olga
So what am I?

Juho
You are umm a *pretty* lady!

Olga
Thanks you!

Juho was just 10 centimetres away from me. I really wanted to be cuddled! I touched the collar of his shirt and pre.tended that I want to remove something from it. This moved him and made him gently touch some strands of my hair. I liked it, so I moved my head closer to have it further fondled. Soon after, he started kissing me passionately for a few minutes nonstop and then suddenly pushed me down on the bed and went on top of me, smashing his lips on mine and forcing his tongue into my mouth. I could clearly hear his breath. Next, he tried to move his hand into my blouse, but the collar of my dress was a bit tight, so I unbuttoned it for him. Afterwards, he held my left bOob. I was pleased to see his pleasure. His compliments made me hot, too, so I forced my hand into my hand bag, and after some blind search, I gave him a love glove! I was happy that he was still into me after all! For about 10 minutes, we became one! One soul in one hybrid body!

Juho had booked another room for himself in the same hotel and had checked in before our arrival.

Olga
Why don't you check out now and stay with us?

He looked excited as if this was what he expected to hear from me!

Juho
Really?!

Olga
Yes!

Juho
I'll do it right now.

Immediately, he went to his room, took his luggage, put it in our room and went ⬇ to check out. While he was out, I took a quick shower. After his arrival, Juho helped me dry and style my hair with a hair dryer. It made me feel so good! He also helped me change Vladimir's clothes. Next, we got ready and walked out to wine and dine. I had a great feeling walking in Helsinki streets. Juho tried to tell me about Finland history, especially in connection with Russia. He also introduced some parts of Helsinki while we were passing by them. During our stay in Helsinki, we visited some touristy attractions of the city. Juho's car had made it convenient to see the city.

On the fourth day, we moved to Tampere. I decided to stay in Juho's flat. It was small but cosy. My presupposition was that Tampere would not be as modern as Helsinki, but I was dead wrong! Juho claimed that almost all cities in Finland more or less enjoy the same facilities as Helsinki does, and Finnish government attempts to provide all parts of the country with necessary services to decentralize.

Olga
Do you have high class and low class areas in Tampere?

Juho
There might be one or two areas in every town that are infamous due to the high number of immigrants or unemployed people living there.

It was strange that areas populated with immigrants were notorious! Are immigrants pests? I asked Juho to take me to one of those infamous areas and then to some areas with good reputation, and he did. In fact, I could not detect huge differences between the houses, infrastructures, streets and looks of those areas at first sight! They looked almost alike, but to me people's *visions* make *di.visions*!

We were in Tampere for three days. During this time, I met Satu, who looked excited to see us. She could not speak English, and Juho served as an interpreter. Kindness overflowed from her smiles, words and gestures. Juho then promised to take me to his hometown next time I visit Finland and meet with his mom.

Soon it was time to de|part. I had a great time with Juho, and I did not want this to end, but neither sad days nor happy days last forever! Everything is ephemeral in this world! Juho took us to the Helsinki train station by his car and pro.mised to visit me in a month or two. I was leaving Finland, and I was leaving my he.art right there! It was hard for me to leave Juho, since a very strong intimate relationship had formed between us in only a few days! However, I had no other choice at that st.age. I was a student and had to finish my studies.

I left Finland with a lump in my throat. We went to pie|ces again. On the way home, I reviewed all moments I spent with Juho, and every now and then, Vladimir interrupted the review process with his cries, smiles or requests. I was in love with Juho, and my love to him doubled after witnessing his affection to Vladimir.

Juho visited us every now and then. In the meantime, he had managed to find more customers in Russia, and he always asked me to accompany him while traveling and visiting his customers in different parts of Russia. I also visited Finland a couple of times, but it was a challenge for me to travel between Russia and Finland, and the climax of this challenge was the time of border crossing. However, our love to each other had truly blurred Finnish Russian border! Our love was an energizer that imparted energy, vitality and spirit to us and made us cross the border frequently, despite its hardships. Love can build a bridge between different peoples. It can blur differences between faces and races, classes and genders, languages and ages!

Soon it was my graduate party. I invited Juho, and he accepted my invitation. I was over the moon. The party went on pretty well; however, it was all in Russian, and every now and then, I looked at Juho to see if he was bored. I received my degree and took some photos with Juho, my family, friends, teachers and classmates. Right there, Juho kneeled down in front of me, and to my great surprise, he popped the question to me!

Juho
Will you marry me?

Olga
Olga

114

I could not believe my eyes! Both Juho and I had become as red as a cherry.

Juho
Will you merry me?

I really didn't know what to say. I was unprepared. In a bashful manner, I looked at my mom's face. She had a smile on, a sign of con10t.

Olga
Olga   **Juho**
Olga   **Juho**
              Juho
Olga
Yes!

My classmates, teachers and friends who did not expect to witness such a scene all cheered up. It was amazing! I never forget those sweet moments! Later, Juho and I went to a restaurant and talked about our plans for our future. Juho wanted me to move to Tampere and live together.

Olga
How about Vladimir?

Juho
He's our son, and I'll serve him like a real dad.

Tears dropped down my eyes, and I cried a river. Juho tried to wipe my tears. My eyes were red and puffy! After hearing his words, I agreed to move to Tampere and cohabit with him. I also shared some of my concerns with him: being a pest that devalues a residential area, finding a job, solving my language barrier, integrating in the new environment, dealing with cultural differences, being away from my mom and brother, to name a few.

Juho listened carefully to my concerns but was hopeful that in a couple of years almost all my concerns are gone! He believed that I look more or less like Finns, so there would not be any problem with me being an immigrant at first sight. He was right, because when I visited Finland, almost everyone spoke to me in Finnish!

Juho
You can attend some Finnish courses. I help you, too, so soon you can shoot your language problem.

That was a good idea; however, later I found that it was not as easy as Juho said. For a couple of years, I at10ded some Finnish courses but no progress. Juho tried to speak to me in Finnish and correct my mistakes, but the pace of my learning was as slow as a snail! For a while, I was depressed, inculcating that I never ever learn this complicated language!

Olga
I'm just wasting my time. I never learn it! It's horrible!

Juho
You will! Harjoitus tekee mestarin!

Olga
How many courses do I need to pass? I have been to different courses for over two years, but I feel I'm still at the first square!

Juho
Don't fret! Go on.

Before long, I found that I was pregnant. Juho was on cloud nine! I had never ever seen Juho happier! However, I was worried! What would happen after our baby is born? Will Juho love Vladimir and care about him after he sees his own real baby?! I was not sure! At the same time, loneliness, joblessness and lack of progress in learning Finnish had made me feel blue. While Juho was at work and Vladimir was in a day care, I felt lonely. Sometimes I thought I could not stand it anymore, and something inside me *pushed* me to return to *Pushkin*. I remembered my past, reviewed my presence and envisaged my future. How the future looks like for me? I was proud of my husband, who was supportive, and this made me calm down when I reached a 10sion point, but anyway, I had studied biology, and I wished to find a relevant job, or at least a job! I did not want to be useless! These concerns had become my company in my l.one.l.iness!

I invited my mom to Finland, and luckily, she arrived a few weeks before my delivery. Her pr.esence replaced the dark clouds of loneliness and despair in my mind with a serene blue sky. She helped me regain my positive energy and hope, and that made my de.live.ry an easier job.

Soon our baby was born, and we named her Suvi! I wanted a Finnish name for Vladimir and myself, too, to avoid receiving some weird reactions we received in a couple of occasions from some

Finns. In fact, Finns are extremely honest. They fail to hide their real feelings, and thus, you can easily read their true emotions from their faces. Perhaps changing our names could help us further camouflage our real identities.

I never forget that once Juho invited a friend of his olden times to a restaurant. Right from the start, Juho's friend talked about Finland Russia relationship from the beginning of history, talking about how Russians have conquered Finland. He then expressed his concerns about the future of Finland, foretelling that finally Russia will swallow Finland if his country does not join NATO! I was shocked! What's that to me? Am I the amb.ass.ador of Russia in Finland? I could feel his strong Russophobe sentiment, anger and aversion from his strong words and red cheeks. For several times, Juho attempted to change the topic of discussion, but his attempts bore no result. Juho's friend did not stop until he emptied himself but filled me!

On the way back home, I saw a driver removing ice from his car windows with a blade. In fact, he was scratching his windows! I was thinking that if he keeps his car in an indoor parking place, or if he uses an interior heater and warms up the car before his trips, the car windows are not frosted. Sometimes we shall take care of our relationships or warm them up to defrost them rather than using a blade and scratch them! Thankfully, Juho and I have proved how love can blur the borders between nations. We reside in one house, sleep on one bed, eat at one table and attempt to clear mis-understandings with the power of love and word.

On the way home, Juho apologized for what happened and tried to soothe me. He told me about the Finland history in relation with Russia – years of oppression which resulted in losing some territories and a future phobia to lose some more! This made me do some research on this issue. According to the poll, conducted by International Gallup Organization in 2004, about 62% of Finns had an anti-Russian sentiment. Since 2014 and after Russia's annexation of *Crime.a*, this sentiment has been even worse in Finland. However, I firmly believe that criticism of the Russian government should not be directed to Russian citizens. Juho is sceptical about the Gallup poll. He laughs and says, "62% of Finns are worried about losing their jobs; 62% of Finns are worried about their favorite ice hockey teams and not Russia."

After a while, I decided to change my name. I informed Juho of my decision, and he had no problem with me changing it. We went through a number of Finnish names together, and after a few days, we chose Sanna. I also adopted Juho's surname. Now I am Sanna Siltamäki. So my form has become Finnish-like; however, my con10t is still Russian.

Form is norm?

Life is form?

Form perform?

Form − con10t = poles − 10t

A letter not sent, a word not meant!

One day, Juho came home happily.

Sanna
You look happy, honey! What's happened?

Juho
I have decided to buy a plot and build our own dream house!

Sanna
Really!? That would be great!

For a while, we had found a great topic for discussion; the size of the house, its form and materials, its plan and design, its location and extent, its shape and color, etc.

We visited some plots offered for sale, but each one of them had at least a defect. Some were far from the city center. Some were malformed. Some had no privacy. Some were too expensive and we could not afford them. Some did not have a nice view. Some had been located near some factories. Some did not have sunshine. Some were not flat. Some were desolate. Nothing is perfect in this world! Sometimes we found some plots that suited us the most, but even before we visit them or talk to house agents, they were sold, and once we managed to make an offer to pur.chase a plot, but another customer offered a higher price and owned it!

After an ex10sive search, which lasted for about 11 months, we found a plot that we thought would suit us the most. Our search revealed that we should not be perfectionists; otherwise, we gain no gain! Soon we started our negotiations with some banks and building companies. Juho and I received some plans based on our budget, but we had some disagreements on our house design. We looked through different house drawings, discussed their defects and removed them to a great ex10t. I believed a house with three bedrooms sufficed, but Juho believed that we should see the future and have four bedrooms. Does he want more babies? Eventually, we reached an agreement and started building it.

Building the house opened my eyes to some realities in Finland. Before it, I always supposed that Finns are *all* very committed, hard-working, honest and fair people; however, after launching the project, I found that Finns are just like other nations. Some are fair, while some are not. To earn more profits, some of them abuse their expertise to overcharge their customers; however, there are some others who offer fair prices for their services. While some are hard-working and punctual, some are not diligent and do not keep their words.

The culmination of this was when we had to choose cabinets for our kitchen, and our building company forced us to choose our kitchen cabinets from the models available in one particular company, active in designing and building cabinets. The designer was horrible. He either refused to attend his workplace, and if he did, he refused to work, and he always had some different pretexts to postpone our work: either he was super-busy, or his computer did not work properly, or he was on vacation, or he was ill. He had more than enough pretexts in his pocket to postpone the work.

Many novel pretexts he had to offer whenever you thought he has run out of them! We were livid with him.

After a month, he eventually made a design and sent it to us by email. We had some comments and contacted him for a face-to-face meeting, but that was like to start from the first square: the repetition and revision of pretexts! After 10 days, we met and applied the comments. He promised to send us the revised design files along with a price list for the extra services. 10 days flew by, and he didn't! He even refused to answer our phone calls and messages. We finally lost it and contacted our building company, and then we found that some other customers have had the same problem with the same cabinet maker!

After about 10 days, he sent us a shocking and vague price list! We talked to some other cabinetmakers, and they all confirmed that he is overcharging us. We started a tough negotiation with him, believing that he has miscalculated some items. At first, he refused to accept it. You know, it is impossible to awaken someone who pretends that he is asleep! Based on our former negotiations and his emails, we finally proved that he has miscalculated some of the costs! What happened after all? He made an apology, but to our surprise, he said that he could not modify the prices! His apology did not ease the 10sion but further exacerbated it! Anyway, his misbehaviors, mistreatments and dishonesty postponed the building project completely for about three months! We faced two more people just like him during the construction process, and they killed our energy, time and joy.

Every now and then, we visited our would-be house and could see its slow progress. In about fifteen months, our new home, which had to be built in nine months, became ready. It was a great feeling to move to our new dream house. We had to buy some beds, furniture, curtains, etc. and install them. This inspired a new feeling in all of us. I love newness. It is a necessity in life. It creates excitement, strength and whim.

With that sense of newness, I decided to improve my Finnish, pass YKI test and apply for citizenship both for myself and Vladimir. I supposed this would make life more convenient for all of us. Sometimes we decided to travel to a country. Juho and Suvi had no problem and could travel there without any visa; however, Vladimir and I needed visa, and this prevented us from traveling to countries that we liked and limited our choices.

For 10 months, I studied hard for the test. Pro.test was an extremely stressful time for me. Sometimes I met with Satu and chitchatted with her in Finnish. She spoke Finnish slowly, formally and clearly, and I could understand her quite well. This helped me build self-confidence in myself.

Finally, it was time for the test. Stress was killing me. On the way, Juho tried to pacify me, but it was of no avail. Stress had nested in my heart and brain, and I failed to break up with it. During the test, stress maxed out, and that negatively affected my capability. I had no control over my mind and even body during the test, and after about 10 minutes, I got sure that I would fail it.

After the test, I left the test location peckishly! Juho was waiting for me in his car. As soon as he saw me, he came toward me excitedly.

Juho
How was your test?

Sanna
Terrible!

Juho
Don't worry! You will pass!

Suddenly, I lost it!

Sanna
Don't try to lull me into hopefulness! Let's stop optimism and live with reality. I don't pass! I had the test, and I know better than anyone else what I've done!

Juho
Juho
Juho

Juho simmered down! He got in the car and drove home. On the way, he did not utter even one single word! This made me feel guilty of conscience. I put him on the pan. Why did I talk to him so angrily? What was his fault? He just wanted to make me feel less 10se. I furtively looked at him. He seemed to be cross with me. He was right. I didn't have any right to talk to him like that!

Sanna
Juho, I'm . . . sorry! I . . . was angry, but still I . . . would have not talked to you . . . like that.

Juho
Juho
Juho

Sanna
Did you hear me?

Juho
Yes!

Sanna
I'm sorry!

Juho
OK!

I was expecting to receive my test result in a couple of months. I had hard times. Failing the test had become a horrible nightmare for me. Every time I opened our post box or saw a mail carrier, my heart sank. I knew that sooner or later I would get a negative result. Juho still tried to stop me feeling di.stressed. He always believes that death is the only problem that has no solution.

The horrible moment I waited for finally arrived. One day, Juho and I returned home. He opened our mailbox and saw an envelope. Its logo was familiar to me more than anyone else in the world.

That was my test result! Quickly, we entered the house. I sat down right in front of the door. I did not dare to open the envelope. I held my breath, closed my eyes and asked Juho to do so.

Juho
Juho
Juho

Myheartwasbeatingfast ∧∧∧∧∧∧∧∧∧∧∧∧∧∧∧∧∧∧∧∧∧∧∧∧∧∧∧

Juho
Onneksi Olkoon!

Sanna
What?!

Juho
Congratulations! Didn't I tell you that you pass!

Sanna
Are you pulling my leg?

Juho
NO! You have passed the test. You have received 3 out of 5 in all skills: listening comprehension 3, writing 3, reading 3 and speaking 3. Well done Sanna!

Sanna
Let me see - - - - - - - - - - Oh my goodness! YES, YES! I passed! How is it possible?

I jumped ↑ and ↓ and cheered up and then hugged Juho!

Sanna
You were right! I should trust your words more hereafter! But I'm sure that examiners have been too lenient; otherwise, I had failed it!

Juho and I started collecting required documents for our citizenship applications. Juho helped me fill in several forms, submit our documents on line and apply for citizenship. Vladimir and I then visited the Tampere police station to confirm the veracity of uploaded documents. Done! We had to wait for seven to eight months to receive the results of our applications.

December 6 is Finland Independence Day, and the great surprise happened to us on December 5 while Finland was celebrating 100 years of its independence! I opened our mailbox and found two envelopes in it among piles of advertisements. The letters had been sent to us by the Finland Police! I hurriedly opened them, and YES! Vladimir and I had received Finnish citizenship!

On December 6, we happily watched Finland's most popular television show, broadcasting the annual reception at the Presidential Palace, wherein the presidential couple stand for several hours and shake hands with about 2000 guests. With funny and weird dresses and hairstyles, some guests become the butt of public laughter. The guest arrangement more or less looks fixed, and thus, several guests attend the event almost every year. While watching it, I was thinking why the president does not use his creativity and make some dramatic changes to this event. Why he spends the tax of Finnish taxpayers for such a celebration, which is limited to several repetitive faces? Why doesn't he invite some other committed members of the society, who serve the nation wholeheartedly, such as ambulance drivers, school teachers, nurses, factory workers, electricians, bus drivers and cleaners? Why only singers, athletes, politicians and cultural activists?! If the president wishes to keep the event as it has been for many years, then he should pay for it from his own salary or receive the expenses back from the humdrums, who wish to continue attending this event and use it for their further fame!

In a little while, I found that I was pregnant again! Juho was extremely happy as if he was becoming a father for the first time in his lifetime. Juho called his mom and informed her. Juho's mom was too happy to hear that. Then, Juho called Satu. We were sure that she would be happy, too, but she did not answer her cell phone. Juho called her again after 10 minutes, but she did not reply.

Juho
Why doesn't she answer her cell phone?

Sanna
I don't know! Perhaps she is in sauna.

Juho called her again, but she did not reply. His eyes glistened with worries! He dressed up quickly and drove to Satu's house. Our new home is about 10 kilometres away from her house. I did not hear from Juho for about an hour. I called Juho a couple of times. First, he did not reply, but then he did.

Sanna
Hi Juho! What's up?

Juho
Hi! I rang her doorbell, and she did not reply. Then, I asked one of her neighbors if they had seen her in the last few days, but they hadn't! I have called the police. They are on their way.

Sanna
I hope she is fine. Keep me posted.

Juho
Sure!

I did not hear anything from Juho for a few hours. I called him over and over again, but he did not reply! This made me worried. I waited for half an hour and called again.

Sanna
Hello Juho! What's up?

Juho
I'm . . . fine!

Sanna
How is Satu?

Juho
Juho

Sanna
I asked how is Satu?

Juho
I'll tell you when I get home.

I could easily feel the depth of grief in his voice.

Sanna
But how is she? Did you find her?

Juho
Satu is . . .

Sanna
What?

Juho went silent for a few ticks. Suddenly, a sob tore at his throat.

Juho
Satu left us!

I was suddenly reduced to tears, and before I hung up the phone, a strangled sob escaped my throat. I cried my eyes out, and this made Suvi wake up! I tried to control myself and put her back to sleep. After a few hours, Juho came back home. His eyes were red and puffy. He could not speak clearly. From his slurred speech, I found that the police has entered Satu's flat, and they had found her *dead* body in her *living* room. It seemed that she had a stroke and had passed away about 10 hours before they arrived!

Before her death, Juho had asked Satu about whether she had any relatives in Finland, and she had given a phone number to Juho. She had only two relatives, living in Kemi and Simo. Juho called them and informed them of Satu's demise. They immediately came to Tampere to arrange a funeral ceremony for her. Juho and I also at10ded her ceremony. How sad it was! Less than 10 people, including priest and his assistants, had at10ded her funeral. I cried but not for Satu. In fact, I cried for myself! How l.one.l.y we have become in the Age of Communication!

Life is so! One day we enter this world, and one day we exit! Upon entering this world, we agree to leave it at any moment it wishes. It can be 1 minute after our arrival, 10 hours or 110 years after. We have come to go! What is important is this: the more time we receive, the more responsibility we have to achieve, and if we do not do something special to improve the lives of other beings, including human beings, animals and plants, we are losers!

The thing I am most afraid of is this: that my coming does not add anything positive to this world; that my life changes nothing and creates nothing as if nobody has come to this world and nothing has happened; that people after me do not find that someone like me has ever lived in this world for a while! I do not want to be like the white pencil in the colored pencil case. It remains untouched even after other colored pencils are used, sharpened and shortened, but the white one leaves no trace, no effect, no impression, no sign, no color, nothing!

Right now, Juho and I are in a hospital for a sonography and check-up. It seems that our next baby is a boy. He is born soon, but what is next? Now that I have a Finnish name and citizenship, will I find a proper job? Will I get rid of loneliness? Will I integrate in my adopted home? Will my plans pan out? Will I leave a trace of myself, or will I be pushed back to Pushkin?

.